DAYS OF WANT SERIES BOOK ONE

T.L. PAYNE

CONTENTS

Chapter 1	1
Chapter 2	12
Chapter 3	19
Chapter 4	25
Chapter 5	32
Chapter 6	39
Chapter 7	46
Chapter 8	56
Chapter 9	66
Chapter 10	73
Chapter 11	79
Chapter 12	84
Chapter 13	90
Chapter 14	97
Chapter 15	109
Chapter 16	117
Chapter 17	121
Chapter 18	126
Chapter 19	134
Chapter 20	144
Chapter 21	151
Chapter 22	157
Chapter 23	164
Chapter 24	172
Chapter 25	180
Chapter 26	190
Chapter 27	194
Chapter 28	203

Also by T. L. Payne   217
Join T. L. Payne on Social Media   219
Acknowledgments   221
About the Author   223

Turbulent

Book One in The Days of Want Series
Copyright © T. L. Payne 2019
All Rights Reserved

Cover design by Deranged Doctor Design
Copy edit by Mia Darien
Proofreading by LKJ Books

www.tlpayne.com
Click here to join the Preferred Reader's Club

OTHER BOOKS BY T. L. PAYNE

Days of Want
Hunted
Turmoil
Uprising
Upheaval
Mayhem
Defiance (Coming summer 2021)
Sudden Chaos

Gateway to Chaos
Seeking Safety
Seeking Refuge
Seeking Justice
Seeking Hope
Seeking Sanctuary (Coming soon!)

Fall of Houston

No Way Out
No Other Choice
No Turning Back
No Surrender
No Man's Land (Coming soon!)

❀ Created with Vellum

CHAPTER 1

Chicago O'Hare International Airport
Chicago, Illinois
Day of Event

Terminal Three of Chicago's O'Hare International Airport was filled with pissed-off passengers. After a four-hour delay, Maddison Langston was feeling cranky herself. Her flight from San Diego had arrived at eleven that morning. By three that afternoon, her connecting flight was still not boarding, even though the plane was at the gate.

When the lights in the terminal cut out and the flight departure screen went blank, Maddie sighed.

Looks like my flight will be delayed. Again.

Sitting in the dim light, Maddie pulled her cell phone from the Silent Pocket Faraday backpack Uncle Ryan had given her. Although she had promised him that she'd keep her phone in the bag while she was in the airport, she was having social media withdrawal. She was not as concerned about a thief scanning her RFID chips as he was.

She pulled the charging cord from the pack and started to plug it into an outlet before realizing that it wouldn't charge with the power off. Maddie tapped a social media app on her phone, but it wouldn't load. Her phone didn't have a signal. After shutting it down and restarting it half a dozen times, it still wouldn't connect to her wireless service provider.

To pass the time, she listened to songs from her music library. She usually listened to her favorite music using streaming services. Luckily, she had a few games on her phone.

Maddie looked up to see an angry man in a sport coat and trousers with one knee on the American Airlines service counter. The terrified woman behind the desk had her back pressed against the wall as far from the out-of-control passenger as possible.

Maddie pulled the earbuds from her ears.

Two men had gripped the arms of the angry man, who was yelling obscenities at the woman, as the woman yelled for security.

"Why can't you tell us what the hell is going on? My flight was supposed to leave three hours ago. Now the lights are out, and it is freaking hot as hell in here," another passenger yelled at the petite woman.

"I do not have anything to tell you. I am in the dark too," she said.

"Oh, is that your attempt to lighten the mood? De-stress the situation? Did they teach you that in customer service school?" the man mocked.

"My cell phone isn't working. I need to use a phone. I have to call my husband. He'll be expecting us to arrive in Nashville any minute," a woman called out.

A tall man in a sports jersey and jeans stepped forward. He towered over the other passengers. Holding an arm up, the man said, "Listen up, folks. All this yelling and getting aggressive with customer service isn't going to get us answers that the woman clearly doesn't have."

"Well, someone sure as hell better start explaining pretty damn fast," the man in the sport coat barked, shaking his arms loose from his captors.

"Look around you. It is a chaotic mess in here. It's not just American Airlines' flights that are delayed. No planes have taken off or landed here in over an hour. The power is out to the airport, and something has disrupted the phones, including cell phones."

Just then, an explosion rattled the windows. The ear-piercing sound of metal on concrete was followed by the cockpit of a jet skidding down the runway. It hadn't occurred to Maddie that planes might collide mid-air without access to tower control for guidance. People rushed from the shopping area of the terminal, dragging their wheeled bags behind them, and huddled near the window to stare at the burning wreckage of the plane on the tarmac.

Maddie slowly rose to her feet. Grabbing her backpack from its position beside her, she flipped it over her shoulder and reached for the extended handle on her suitcase. The terminal was in darkness, lit only by the windows where a surreal show of flames and black smoke was casting long shadows toward the center of the concourse.

As Maddie stared out the window with her mouth open wide at the flaming, smoking, twisted mass, a second Boeing 737 dropped from the sky in pieces, scattering onto the runway and bursting into flames. The lights were out, there was no cell service, and planes were colliding in the sky above them.

Maddie came to a startling realization. It had happened. The EMP—the electromagnetic pulse—her dad and Uncle Ryan talked about had really happened. Her hand shot up to cover her mouth. Maddie's feet would not move, even though her brain said run.

She couldn't catch her breath. While her fellow travelers stood with eyes peeled to the horrid sight and their mouths wide in shock and terror, Maddie ran.

Her bag's wheels skipped off the floor of the concourse as Maddie bolted toward a family restroom. Her backpack smacked the wall as she spun around to turn the lock. Maddie dropped her pack and suitcase by the door and slid to the cold tile floor. Hugging her knees to her chest, she sobbed, rocking side to side. Mixed with the crushing fear was a pang of guilt. She had mocked her dad for his paranoia. A wave of grief threatened to crash over her without mercy. As she cried, the years of repressed grief burst to the surface as she recalled the training and warnings her father had tried to communicate to her over the years.

Maddie hadn't cried this much since the accident. The day her dad died. The day her world changed forever.

As the tears flowed in torrents, Maddie rested her head on her arms. She was startled by loud banging behind her. She jumped to her feet and spun to face the door, her heart pounding against her chest. In the blackness, she couldn't see her hand in front of her face. Maddie pulled her phone from her back pocket and activated its flashlight feature. Holding it over her head, she turned and looked around the small room.

I can't stay in here forever.

How long before a plane came crashing through the terminal? How many were up there circling the airport? How many had diverted from their flight paths to land after they lost their navigation system and contact with the control tower? Pilots would only have line-of-sight to avoid a mid-air collision. How soon would it be before they ran out of fuel? Maddie's thoughts raced.

She had to get some place safe right now. That was what her dad always told her. The longer she hesitated, the more dangerous it would be.

Maddie stood and blew her nose. She bent over to reach for her pack.

She froze.

Maddie's heart dropped. She was stranded in one of the country's busiest airports in the middle of one of the most populated cities. And she had never felt more alone.

Maddie turned and put her back to the door. She slid once more to the floor, curling her arms over her head.

Dad was right.

Her friends had called her father, Greg Langston, a doomsday prepper—a title that brought Maddie embarrassment. Before he died, her father had taught her and her brother, Zach, survival skills and how to prepare for disasters. She never took it as seriously as she should have.

"What do I do, Daddy? What do I do?" she cried.

Her mind raced, searching for answers. Images of her rolling her eyes as her dad lectured her and Zach on what to do in a world-ending scenario brought a new round of guilt and shame.

"You were right, Daddy. I am so sorry I mocked you. I didn't listen to you, and now the shit has hit the fan, and I don't know what to do."

She curled into a fetal position. Time seemed to stand still in the tiny, cold room. She stared at the shadow cast by her cell phone. Her mind went blank. She slid into a familiar numbness. Sleep had been her comfort, her only solace in the days and weeks after her dad died. She wanted to go there. She let her breathing slow.

She was shaken back to reality by the sound of the growing chaos outside the bathroom.

Maddie heard her dad's voice in her head.

"Maddison Grace Langston, pay attention. Someday, you might find yourself alone when the shit hits the fan and you will need to know how to survive and get home."

She sat up, brushing loose strands of hair from her face.

The get-home bag her dad had given her containing all the essentials to survive on the road was in her dorm room in Ohio. It would do her no good now. But she had the everyday-carry items with her. Uncle Ryan had picked up where her dad left off in making sure carrying her EDC was a habit. Maddie looked down at the plain, waterproof backpack on the floor next to her. There were times in the last few years when she had resented Ryan for trying to take her dad's place. At that moment, she was grateful he had.

Maddie got to her feet and walked over to the sink. She looked in the mirror. Mascara streaked her face, and her hazel eyes were bloodshot. She ran her hand through her long, blonde hair, pulling it into a messy bun on top of her head and securing it with the hair tie from her wrist. She stared at herself in the mirror.

"You've got this, Maddie. You can do it."

She pointed to the mirror with her index finger.

You have to.

Unzipping her carry-on bag, Maddie was relieved that she had brought her hydration pack on the trip. Knowing she'd need to run every day to maintain her current level of endurance, she had thrown it in her bag. Pulling the vest pack from her suitcase and emptying all the pockets and pouches, she quickly inventoried its contents. With the Jelly Belly Sport Beans, sports gels, and energy bars, she had about ten thousand calories with her. Her hydration bladder and water flasks held at least two liters of water. She added the weight up in her head. She'd be carrying around ten pounds.

When running a marathon or endurance race, she didn't take the hydration bladder or as many energy gels. There was an aid station along the route, and her crew would take position between stations in case she needed a quick pick-me-up. But Maddie had carried that much weight when she did backcountry and trail runs, so she knew she could.

In a Ziploc bag were two headlamps, extra batteries, a compass, and a multifunction mini tool—all requirements from her last race. From her every-day carry pack, she removed the emergency bivvy bag, her Sawyer MINI water filter, and a LifeStraw personal water filter. Maddie shoved them into the kangaroo pouch of her vest pack, along with a Ziploc bag of socks and thermals. The last thing in was a weatherproof jacket.

Maddie undressed and pulled on her running tights. After putting on a tank top, she put on a fresh pair of socks and slid on her running shoes. She wished she hadn't chosen to bring the red ones. They would stand out too much, but there was nothing she could do about that now.

Gathering up the water flasks and bladder, Maddie filled them in the sink. She pushed the bladder into the pouch and placed it in the hydration vest pack.

Placing her arms through the arm holes of the vest, she adjusted the straps across her chest. Her runner's pack was a vest-style. It wrapped around her, fitting snugly against her body. She tugged on the cords. It felt secure. After placing the soft flasks in the front pockets, she strapped one squeeze flask to her wrist. Lastly, she pulled on her dad's Marine Corps Marathon head-band and adjusted it to cover her ears.

She looked down at the half-empty suitcase and her clothes strewn about the floor. She picked them up and threw them into the bag. Maddie didn't consider herself overly materialistic, but her suitcase contained some of her favorite clothes. It pained her to just leave them there.

This is crazy. How am I going to run all the way to St. Louis?

From her Silent Pocket Faraday backpack, Maddie retrieved her earbuds, car keys, and a pack of gum. As she placed them in the right-side pocket, her hands shook so badly that she dropped her car keys on the floor. She was alone in Chicago and the end of civilization as she knew it had occurred—just as her dad had predicted. She was scared shitless and was not afraid to admit it. Maddie shook her head, attempting to fight back the tears that threatened to spill down her face.

Harden up, Maddie.

No one was coming to save her. If she was going to make it,

she'd have to protect herself. She couldn't afford to let self-doubt and indecision keep her prisoner in the airport.

St. Louis was about three hundred miles away. The previous week, she had run the New Hampshire 100-mile endurance race in twenty-six hours. So, with needing recovery time between runs, it would take at least a week or more to get home.

How long will it take if I have to avoid dangerous people?

She wanted nothing more than to sit back down on the cold tile floor, curl into a ball, and stay there until her mom came to her rescue.

Mom is not coming, Maddie. Mom is stranded in California.

She had gone with her mother to San Diego. They had brought her grandmother home from the hospital. Her mother wanted Grand to enjoy her last days at home in her own bed surrounded by the things she loved, including her one-eyed dog, Jack. The sudden realization that her mom might not be able to make it back home to Missouri shook her to her core. She had been so focused on herself that she hadn't even thought about where her mom and brother were. When she had last received a text message from Zach, he had been coming back from his school field trip to Washington, D.C.

Maddie placed her hands over her face and rubbed her forehead.

Where did he say they had stopped?

Maddie retrieved her cell phone from the floor beside her suitcase, opened her messages app, and clicked on the last message from Zach. He had been in Marshall, Illinois, right before the lights went out.

Maybe the lights aren't out there?

Although she was unsure where Marshall, Illinois, was, she doubted it was anywhere near Chicago. His bus had been heading southwest back to St. Louis.

He will be all right. There were six teachers on the trip. They'll get him home.

She checked for cell service one last time before putting her phone in the front pouch of her vest. The light from the phone shined through the mesh fabric. She patted her pockets, adjusted her straps, and pulled the cords tight.

Time to get going.

Maddie slowly unlocked and cracked opened the door. The scene out in the corridor was even more chaotic than before. She could hear raised voices and crying.

How long was I in there?

She checked her watch. It was four o'clock. She had at least two hours before it would be dark. Walking down the terminal toward the main hall, she could see that most of the activity centered on the restaurant area of the concourse. People were fighting over what was left of the food.

She needed a map. She had seen a place that sold books and newspapers when she'd gotten coffee earlier.

They should have maps. There are tourists here, right?

Maddie raced around a corner and saw a floor to ceiling mural of the city of Chicago. It wouldn't replace a paper map that she could take with her, but it would give her a direction to head out in at least. Not knowing the scale of the map, she made a fist and stuck up her thumb, using it as a ruler to calculate distance.

"Which way are you heading?" a man asked.

The voice startled her, causing her to jump. She twirled around to find a man in his mid-thirties. Beside the man stood a woman, maybe a little younger than him, and a girl of about ten years old.

"Um— I— South," Maddie stammered.

She chastised herself. She had just given out critical information to a stranger. She could hear her father scold her.

OPSEC, Maddie, her dad would say.

Operational security meant keeping your big trap shut about what you have and where you plan to go. She was sucking at this already. She looked at her feet.

"Your dad serve?" the man asked, pointing to Maddie's Marine Corps buff.

"He did. Did you?" she asked, pointing to the U.S. Army National Guard Minute Man logo on his hat.

"I did."

"Two tours in Iraq and four in Afghanistan," the woman added.

"Yeah, my dad spent a lot of time in those places too."

"Is he with you?" the man asked.

Maddie looked away and swallowed hard, resolved to fight back the tears. She'd give anything to have her dad with her right now.

"I'm Rob Andrews, by the way, and this is my wife April and our daughter Emma."

Emma gave a timid wave as April stepped forward and extended her hand. Maddie shook it and said, "I'm Maddie Langston."

"Look, it is getting bad in here. It's going to get worse in the city very soon. We're not going to wait around for the lights to come back on. We're getting out of here, and it looks like you have the same idea," Rob said.

"Um... Yeah. I mean, I was thinking about it. With the airplanes crashing, I was trying to decide how to leave to avoid the runways. I need to head toward Interstate 55, but that is southwest, and it looks like most of the runways are in that direction."

"You could go due south and then cut over, say, around here." Rob pointed to 143rd Street on the map mural.

"I wish I had a map to take with me, in case I have to adjust course quickly."

"I have a map. We're heading south too. We live about fifty miles from here. You're welcome to join us until you need to head west."

"I don't know if I should."

"You shouldn't be out on the streets alone. It's not safe on a regular day, but now with the power being out..."

Maddie was leery of leaving the airport with strangers, but he was right. It wasn't safe to go alone. Safety in numbers, as her dad would say.

She looked the man over. He had been in the military like her dad. He had his wife and daughter with him.

It should be all right, right?

"Okay. When do you want to leave?"

CHAPTER 2

San Diego, California
Day of Event

Beth's drive back to her mother's house after dropping off her eighteen-year-old daughter at the San Diego airport was difficult. The doctor had put her mother on hospice care just days before. She hadn't had time to adjust to the news that her mother would not recover from cancer this time.

Beth's mother, Florence, had beaten breast cancer twice. The third time, it was in her bones. Her mother was sixty-eight and had led a full, vibrant, active life before this most recent diagnosis.

The traffic was heavy—heavier than Beth remembered from when she had lived there before marrying her first husband, Greg Langston. But that was ages ago. She had lived all over since then, settling in Missouri. When Greg left the Marines and took the job in St. Louis, Beth had been thrilled.

For the first time in their marriage, they had been able to settle in the place of their choosing. To be honest, though, St. Louis hadn't been her first choice. She could think of much nicer places to live, but Greg had received a great job offer from a military defense contractor. The job allowed him to be home with Beth and their children, Maddie and Zach.

Beth pulled the car into the third bay of her parents' three-car garage. She unloaded the groceries and placed them on the marble countertop.

"Beth, is that you?"

"Yes, Mom, it's me. Can I bring you some juice? I stopped at Panera Bread and bought you some of the chicken and wild rice soup you like."

"Maybe later, dear. I…"

She was getting weaker and sleeping longer. Beth wasn't sure if it was because of the cancer or the pain meds. She was incoherent a lot when she was awake. Beth had moved the dining table and china cabinet out of the dining room to set her mother's hospital bed up there. Her stepfather, Frank, was set up in the den, where he spent most of his time. He had suffered a stroke the year before, leaving his left arm paralyzed.

Beth finished putting the groceries away and went into the den to check on Frank.

"Frank, can I get you some soup or a sandwich?"

He didn't answer, so she said it louder. The television was blaring, so she had to yell to be heard over the commentator's gloomy newscast.

"Frank," she yelled.

"What? Why are you yelling at me?" Frank asked, glowering over his shoulder.

He turned back to stare at the television before she could finish her sentence. She rolled her eyes and went back to the kitchen.

"I'll just make him a tray, and if he's hungry, he'll eat it," she said out loud, exasperated.

"What did you say?" Frank called from the den.

Beth shook her head and pulled a bowl from the cabinet next to the sink. She made Frank a tray and set it on the coffee table in front of him.

"You're blocking the television," Frank barked, craning his neck around her.

China's president, Xi Jinping, is said to have facilitated the talks between North Korean leader Kim Jong Un and the United States. U.S. State Department spokesman, Robin Payton, said Monday that the president had rejected calls from China, Russia, and North Korea to lift sanctions imposed on the isolated state. The U.S. remains committed to only doing so when Pyongyang makes further progress toward denuclearization on the Korean Peninsula. Further talks between Chairman Kim and President Rhynard have yet to be scheduled.

"You can't trust those damn commie North Koreans. Are they nuts or something? What the hell are we talking to them for anyway," Frank yelled at the television.

Beth had never been so tired of listening to the news in her life.

Why in the world did they invent twenty-four-hour news stations, anyway? All they do is repeat the same bad news over and over.

～

Sandy, the hospice nurse, arrived shortly after one o'clock that afternoon. She took Florence's vitals and adjusted her morphine pump.

"She is sleeping most of the time now. Is it from the meds?" Beth asked as she walked Sandy to her car.

"Her urine output has decreased again. I increased her fluids, but I think her kidneys are shutting down."

The nurse put a hand on Beth's shoulder. Her eyes were full of sympathy.

"It is just a matter of days now—maybe three or four. If you have family to call in, I'd say now would be the time. She'll likely slip into a coma in a day or two."

Beth inhaled and held it. She had known those words were coming. She had felt it in her heart, and she'd thought she was prepared for it. Beth thanked Sandy and walked back into the house. All she wanted to do was go upstairs to her room, crawl into bed, and pull up the covers. That was what she had done after her husband, Greg had died. She had shut down. Sleep was her only comfort. She didn't have the luxury of retreat today, however. She had ill parents and a lazy, one-eyed dog to care for.

Jack slept in the bed with Beth's mother. He rarely left her side. She stroked the dog's head as she stared down at her mom. He lifted his head, shifted position, then put his head on Florence's leg. Feeling sorry for her mother's furry child, she decided she'd reheat the chicken and rice she had made him the day before.

"Jack, you want some lunch?"

Jack's paws hit the wood floor, and a flash of white fur streaked by her feet. Jack loved food.

"What are we going to do with you, little guy?"

She hated the thought of taking him to an animal rescue, but her husband, Jason, would never allow her to bring him home with her. They already had a dog he didn't like.

As Beth followed Jack into the kitchen, an ear-piercing emergency alert tone came from Frank's television. Beth's first thought was the alert was for a wildfire. They hadn't had rain in a while. Beth placed the kitchen towel she held in her hand onto the counter and walked into the den just as the emergency alert message began to scroll across the screen.

We interrupt our programming. This is a national emergency. The Department of Homeland Security has issued a national emergency alert. Residents are asked to shelter in place until further notice. Stay tuned to this channel for updates. This is not a test.

Beth heard the alert tone on her cell phone and ran to the kitchen to retrieve it.

Presidential Alert

THIS IS NOT A TEST. This is a national emergency. Shelter in place until further notice.

"What the hell?" Frank said.

Beth clicked the news app on her phone to check for news about the emergency alert but found none. She opened the Facebook app and scrolled through the messages. She stared down at her phone as her news feed refreshed. A story from a San Diego station informed the city that the nation had been attacked. Beth dropped to her knees, her cell phone skidding across the floor. Crawling over to pick it back up, she leaned against the kitchen cabinets and read the article.

San Diego Daily News has been informed that at approximately twenty-three minutes past three this afternoon, a nuclear device exploded in the atmosphere above the United States. Information is still coming in regarding the extent of the damage this detonation has caused and the areas affected. But right now, we know that communications with most of the nation have been interrupted. An official with the governor's office has told Daily News that they have no information regarding further attacks. A state of emergency has been declared, and residents have been ordered to shelter in place until further notice. We expect a formal statement from the governor later today. Stay tuned for further details.

Beth kept scrolling through her news feed, hoping for more news. She tapped on contacts, selected Maddie's cell number, and pressed the call button. The call failed, so she couldn't even leave a voicemail. She opened her message app and typed a message to Maddie and Zach, then tapped the send button. She waited. A moment later, a message appeared telling her that delivery had failed.

Beth buried her head in her hands. Being cut off from her children during a national emergency was beyond any heartache she had ever experienced. Rocking back and forth, she tried to control her panic. She repeatedly tapped the message's send button, hoping desperately that it would go through.

Placing her hands on the counter, Beth pulled herself to her feet. She ran her hands through her hair. Her mind wanted to go numb, but she couldn't give in to that. Walking over to the sink, she washed her face and dried off with a kitchen towel. She heard a news anchor discussing the shelter in place order and headed back to the den.

Frank was unusually quiet as he and Beth sat staring at the television screen. All anyone could say was that no one knew what the damage was throughout the rest of the country. All planes had been grounded, and a state-wide curfew had been ordered. No one was allowed out of their homes except essential personnel.

It was hours before news reports came in about the blackout caused by the EMP. A so-called expert explained the effects of an EMP detonated at a three-hundred-mile altitude. As far as they had determined, the unaffected areas include parts of California, Oregon, Washington, and Alaska. Beth didn't need to listen to the rest. She understood the effects of an EMP. Her deceased husband, Greg had studied it as one of the possible scenarios he foresaw happening.

She was cut off from her children and her current husband, Jason. She was two thousand miles away, and there was nothing she could do to protect them. Worse yet, they were both away from home and separated from each other. Zach would have his teachers for help and support, but Maddie was stranded in an airport in a large, densely-populated city.

Beth paced the room. No matter how hard she tried, she couldn't think of a single thing she could do to help her children or even try to get to them. The roads were shut down. The authorities wern't allowing anyone to travel. Walking two thousand miles without any gear was impossible.

"Beth? Where are you, Beth?"

"I'm right here, Mom. I'm coming."

No matter how desperately she wanted to get home to her children, she knew she could not leave her dying mother, and it would be foolish to go alone anyway. She wouldn't make it out of California, let alone across four states of chaos and devastation.

Even though every cell in her body wanted to get to her children, she'd have to stay there and care for her parents.

CHAPTER 3

Chicago O'Hare International Airport
Chicago, Illinois
Day of Event

As the Andrews family prepared to leave the airport, Maddie studied the map on the wall. Although she was relieved she wouldn't be heading out alone, she was worried that they'd slow her down.

An explosion rattled the windows as a third plane crashed to the ground, skidded down the runway, and slid into the wreckage, its fire flooding light into the dim concourse. Maddie shot to her feet and ran toward Rob and his family.

We need to get out of here now!

Maddie stopped short and watched as the family huddled in panic over their suitcases.

"We can't wheel all these suitcases fifty miles down the middle of the crowded streets. Stranded motorists will be flooding the roads and sidewalks by now," Rob said, placing his hand on his wife's suitcase.

"You can leave all your things here if you want," April said. "It won't fit in any of our backpacks or my tote, and I can't carry it around in my arms. What if someone knocks it from my hands? I am not leaving it, and that is final."

Maddie tapped her fingertips on her legs and looked over her shoulder at the wreckage.

"Rob... We have to go now," Maddie said.

Rob tried to take the suitcase from April.

"Emma can't pull her suitcase fifty miles, so it is staying here. I'll probably be carrying her part of the way."

"I'm not leaving it, Rob." April said, pulling the handle from her husband's grasp.

Rob stepped back, bumping into Emma. Emma turned and tripped over her bag. Rob reached out and caught her, lifting her off her feet and giving her a quick squeeze before putting her down.

Maddie's heart ached. Her dad wasn't there to catch her when she fell. That huge safety net had been missing since she was fifteen. She'd give anything for him to be there to catch her right then. She wondered if Emma knew how lucky she was to have her dad with her in this mess.

April reached down and brushed strands of curls from Emma's eyes.

Rob reached down and grabbed the handle of April's suitcase. April glared at him.

"I'll take it. You can't carry it, April, and there are going to be places that you can't roll it. If we're going to have a chance of making it home, you need to let me carry it."

"No, you'll leave it somewhere."

"I promise, April, I'll do my very best."

"No, Rob, I can do it."

Rob shook his head and walked away, leaving the bag with April.

Maddie continued to tap her fingers on her legs as she watched him go. She looked to the main hallway and back to Rob. She wondered what the security personnel were doing. Earlier, she had seen a group of them running toward terminal two, but besides the useless customer service people, no one had come to tell anyone what they should do.

No sooner had the question popped into her mind than two airport security officers appeared. One of the officers climbed onto a chair.

"Folks, if I can have your attention..." he said.

The crowd began to quiet and gather near the security officers.

"It's about time someone came to tell us what the hell is going on around here. Why are the lights out, and why are planes crashing?" a man yelled.

"Are we safe in the airport? Is someone coming to get us out of here?" another yelled.

"If you will quiet down, I'll tell you what we know. All right?"

The security officer paused and waited for the passengers to quiet.

"All right. At 3:15 p.m. today, the President of the United States declared a national emergency and ordered everyone to shelter in place. That—"

Questions from the crowd interrupted his announcement. He held a hand up and waited for everyone to quiet down again.

"If you'll stop interrupting me, I'll finish my announcement and then answer your questions to the best of my ability."

He paused.

"The order to shelter in place means that at this time, no one is allowed to travel."

The crowd grew loud again, and the officer waited.

"Everyone just shut the hell up and let the officer tell us what is going on. If you keep interrupting and shouting him down, none of us are going to find out what is happening," a man in the crowd yelled.

After the crowd quieted, the security officer continued.

"From what little we know right now, it seems that our country has come under some type of attack."

People murmured. Some held their hands over their mouths. Looks of shock and disbelief were evident on everyone's faces.

"Communications are down now, but right before the electricity went off, we received a message from Homeland Security about the shelter in place order. We're doing everything we can to find out more, but as of right now, we've been unable to contact anyone outside the airport. As such, we must enforce the order until such time as it is rescinded by the president. All airport exits are locked, and no one is allowed to leave at this time."

Passengers began shouting, and the crowd began pushing in on the two security officers. The man stepped down from the chair, and he and the other officer ran off down the main hall of the terminal with much of the crowd in tow.

As the remainder of the crowd dispersed, Maddie could see fear on their faces. Maddie ran over to Rob, who was hurrying back to his family. Across the terminal, a twenty-something man in a tank top and shorts was shaking the steel roll-down gate at the coffee shop. All the stores had been closed up, and the stranded travelers were increasingly voicing their displeasure with that fact. The vending machines were empty.

When Maddie caught up with Rob, she grabbed his arm. As he turned toward her, Maddie heard a loud banging. She stumbled, but Rob caught her. They turned in unison to see a crowd growing at the bagel shop, and they had been successful in prying open the security gate. The throng of people pushed and shoved their way into the shop. Angry voices and the crashing of tables being thrown came from the store. Seconds later, mothers were fleeing with their children clutched to their chests. It had only been a few hours since the lights had gone out, and people were already looting and willing to fight each other over a bagel.

Maddie looked at Rob wide-eyed.

"It's time to get out of here. If it's this bad in here, I hate to see how it is outside on the streets," Rob said, turning toward his family.

"I agree, but how do we get around security? They've locked down the exits." Maddie said.

"Now that they have told everyone what's going on, there will be a mass exodus. They'll have a difficult time handling all the people. We need to go now, while they're occupied with all the unhappy people. We need to find an exit they haven't locked."

"That's what I was thinking," Maddie said, bending over to tighten the laces on her running shoes.

She was glad that she had remembered to replace the laces with paracord. It was a habit from her hiking days with her family, but she liked having the extra strong laces when she ran as well. It really sucked to break a shoelace during a marathon and have to limp to the aid station with a shoe flopping.

As she made the loops with the paracord to tie her shoes, her hands shook. Blowing out her cheeks, she let out the breath she had been holding. The sound of her heart beating thrashed in her ears. She managed to finish tying her shoelaces and looked over to the crowd that was slowly exiting the bagel shop.

She considered staying in the airport and waiting for her mom, stepdad, or someone to come to rescue her. The thought of walking through scenes like the Ferguson riots terrified her. Images of people being pulled from their vehicles by angry mobs flashed through her mind. She recalled the images on television of hooded men throwing Molotov cocktails at store windows.

As she straightened up, she felt faint. Her legs felt weak. But she knew she shouldn't give in to fear.

No, I need to get home.

Dad said never to wait because things would only get worse as society crumbled. I have to make it out of Chicago.

"I just need to stay with the Andrews and make it through the burbs," she murmured to herself.

You can do this, Maddie, her dad's voice said inside her head.

I hope so, Daddy. I truly hope so.

CHAPTER 4

Interstate 70
Marshall, Illinois
Day of Event

When the Beckett Hall High School bus pulled into a McDonald's parking lot just off Interstate 70 in Marshall, Illinois, Zach Langston and his classmates were still hours away from making it home from a field trip to Washington, D.C. While the other students headed inside the restaurant, Zach stayed outside to check in with his mother and send a text to his sister. He pocketed his phone, picked up his pack, and went into the restaurant, taking his place in line behind his best friends, Jacob Morton and Connor Haas.

"Dude, why do you carry that heavy-ass pack everywhere you go? You have your molly in there or something?" Jacob asked, slapping Zach on the shoulder.

After picking up their food, Zach, Jacob, and Connor took their meals to a table outside. Zach and his friends were in a fierce debate about who was stronger, Captain Marvel or Wonder

Woman, when the sound of grinding metal and shattering glass interrupted their conversation.

~

The boys stood to get a better look. Cars were piled up like cordwood in the intersection, and more cars plowed into the wreckage. Smoke billowed from the heap, and people spilled out of the restaurant to gawk at the scene.

"What happened?" a girl asked.

"The lights are out. The traffic lights aren't working," another voice in the crowd said.

"Did someone call 911?"

"I tried, but my phone is dead."

"I had service a minute ago, but my phone is dead too," another girl called.

There was a flurry of movement as Zach, Jacob, Connor, and the other kids pulled their phones out to check them.

"Anyone have cell service?" Mr. Dean asked.

Everyone shook their heads.

Mr. Dean walked over to Zach's table and stared at the wreckage.

"What do you think, Mr. D?" Jacob asked.

All the students at the private college preparatory school loved Mr. Dean—even kids who didn't have his classes liked him.

"I'm not sure, Jacob. Must be a storm somewhere that took out a transformer station. That could take out a cell tower, maybe," Mr. Dean said.

A round man in his late sixties stepped out of his car and looked around the parking lot.

"Anyone have jumper cables? My car won't start," the man said.

A woman in an SUV two spots over poked her head out of her car door and said, "My car isn't working either."

Getting to his feet, Zach looked to Mr. Dean.

Zach's heart plummeted. Reaching down, he snagged his pack off the bench. He was just about to heave it over his shoulder when Mr. Dean grabbed his arm.

"Don't, Zach. Wait. We have to be certain."

"There's only one thing I know of that can knock out cell phones, cause a power outage, and make cars quit working all at the same time."

"Shush, Zach. We don't want to start a panic. We came here as a group. We need to stick together. Just hold on and I'll make sure we all make it home."

"But my dad always said…"

"I understand, but we aren't near a big city. Look around. This is the extent of the commercial businesses."

Looking around, Zach saw only a Walmart Super Center and a gas station. There wasn't much else.

"If it is an EMP, it is not going to get better with time—only worse. I want to be home by then," Zach said.

Lowering his pack onto the chair, Zach ran his arm through the strap, ready to grab it and run. He wasn't sure how quickly things would go to hell, but he wasn't going to let his guard down. Unlike his mother and sister, he believed everything his dad had said about the need to be prepared. He had been eleven when his dad had died—not old enough to understand all the political stuff his dad talked about, but he'd researched it since his death. He'd read the books in his dad's office. He had taken them before his mom boxed everything up when they moved in with his stepdad.

The crowd in the parking lot grew. It seemed everyone somehow sensed something different about the power outage, and their voices were full of fear. Zach had read that when people's ability to communicate and move freely was taken from them, it can cause a sense of powerlessness. That kind of fear was danger-ous. The fear of what could happen next could make some people to panic and do things they usually wouldn't.

"Bro, this blows. I have plans with Zoe Lambert tonight. Who knows what time we will get home now," Connor said.

Although Zach wanted to tell him the bad news, he refrained. Connor wouldn't believe him. Before, when Zach tried sharing his thoughts on being prepared with Jacob and Connor, they'd looked at him like he was crazy.

"Zach, we're going to move everyone back onto the bus. It'll be easier to keep track of everyone," Mr. Dean said.

Zach nodded and picked up his pack, heading toward the bus.

"All right, everyone, listen up. All Beckett Hall students and faculty, please make your way back to the bus," Mr. Dean called.

After giving his name to the teacher with the clipboard, Zach boarded the bus. He returned to his seat in the back next to the rear door. He stepped over Jacob and Connor's backpacks and flopped into a seat. When Jacob and Connor boarded the bus, Zach stood and let them have the window and middle positions. No way was he being trapped against the window and have to crawl over his friends to escape, if needed.

"Damn. I sure hope we aren't trapped on this freaking bus all afternoon. This is boring as hell. I can't even listen to music," Connor said.

As Zach stared out the window, he noticed the crowd of people in the parking lot had grown. The occupants of the cars from the intersection had joined the group from Walmart and McDonald's.

"Hey, Connor, lower that window, man. It's freaking hot as hell in here," Jacob said.

Jacob nudged Zach with his elbow.

"Or is that Zach over here with the hots for Makayla?"

Zach punched Jacob in the arm. Jacob bent over, clutching his injury.

"Damn, boy, no call for violence just because I speak the truth," Jacob said in a low voice.

Zach resisted the urge to look up to see if Makayla had heard him. Jacob could be such a dick sometimes.

After hours stranded on the bus in the McDonald's parking lot, Mr. Dean allowed the students bathroom breaks in the restaurant. They went in two at a time and for only five minutes. The restaurant manager had shut down food service but was still allowing them to use the facility.

When the manager discovered that the lights weren't coming back on, he'd have a hell of a time getting all those people to leave. The lone sheriff's deputy that had shown up on a four-wheeler to keep the peace sure wouldn't be much help if the crowd got ugly.

The crowd in the parking lot became more agitated. A uniformed policeman joined the deputy. The frustrated mob demanded answers from the officers—answers they didn't have or would not give.

"Now, folks, settle down and listen to me. We don't know any more about what is going on with the lights than you do. Our communication systems are down, but I have sent an officer to Ameren Electric to find out when they'll get the power back on. As soon as I know something to tell you folks, I will. Until then, sit tight until we get the word."

Mr. Dean made his way through the crowd and approached the officer. The two men spoke, then Mr. Dean returned to the bus.

"Okay, everyone, settle down. It appears they still don't know what caused the power outage or the vehicles to stop working, but the chief says that they have a plan in place for an emergency shelter if it doesn't come back on soon. So, sit tight a little longer."

Zach wanted off the bus. He knew he should have already been on the road home, and he was kicking himself for letting Mr. Dean talk him into staying. But he trusted his teacher. He hoped he wouldn't regret it.

As the chief of police delivered the bad news about the attack and subsequent shelter-in-place order from the president to the weary crowd gathered in the McDonald's parking lot, many stared in disbelief while others grumbled.

"This here is Reverend Williams. He has been gracious enough to open his church for those of you stranded by this event. You'll be provided with a cot, food, and water. We ask that, for your safety, everyone remain in the church for the duration of the emergency. The sheriff has sent men to Decatur to get in touch with the Federal Emergency Management folks for answers as to what they are doing to help stranded travelers. We expect to have answers for you tomorrow evening."

There were quite a few groans and murmurs in the crowd, but for the most part, everyone listened in silence. Once the police chief was finished speaking, he turned the meeting over to the reverend.

"Good evening. I am Reverend Williams with the Olive Street Christian Church. We have wonderful volunteers who have set up cots in the basement of our church and sanctuary for you fine folks. It is only three blocks from here, but if anyone needs assistance walking, please raise your hand. We will see what we can do to provide a wheelchair. If everyone else would please follow Brother Michaels over there, he's the one with the red and white banner."

Zach looked to Mr. Dean, who must have read Zach's mind, because he shook his head and walked over.

"Don't do it, Zach. It is too far to go on foot. I have to stay here and make sure the rest of your classmates get home safe. You can't go out there alone. That is just crazy."

"But—"

"It's going to get crazy out there. I can't let you head off by yourself, Zach. I'm responsible for you. You don't want to get me fired, do you?"

Zach stared at Mr. Dean. He didn't want to go stay in some

church basement waiting for things to get worse. When the town's residents received word that the power was not coming back on and food delivery trucks wern't coming to restock their groceries, he knew they'd turn on the stranded travelers. He didn't want to get Mr. Dean fired, though. His shoulders slumped, and Zach followed his teacher to the line forming behind the minister.

CHAPTER 5

FEMA Region Five Offices
  Federal Building
  Chicago, Illinois
  Day of Event

The conference room rumbled with nervous voices. Within three hours of the president issuing a national emergency, Regional Administrator Reginald Harding had called together his staff to coordinate response and recovery efforts. As he entered the room, all eyes fell on him as he took his seat at the head of the conference table.

"Okay, everyone, I am going to do my best to tell you what we know so far, which I must confess is damned little. At this point, we do know that our country has come under coordinated attacks from Russia, China, Iran, and North Korea. At approximately fifteen-hundred hours today, defense radar picked up two intercontinental ballistic missiles launched from North Korea and directed at the mainland of the United States."

The room erupted in panicked voices. Some rose to their feet while others sat silently with their hands covering their mouths.

"Please, everyone, settle down. I know this is quite a shock to us all, but we have too much to do to fall apart now," Harding said.

After a moment, the room quieted, and the administrator continued.

"North Korea's missiles were shot down by Ground-based Midcourse Defense, with none making it to their targets."

Everyone in the room let out a sigh of relief.

"However, as we focused our response on North Korea, we came under coordinated attacks from Russia, China, and Iran. Multiple ballistic missiles were launched from those countries. The first were anti-satellite missiles. A nuclear missile was detonated over the United States, setting off an EMP. The electromagnetic pulse has taken down the power grid, communications, and transportation to most of the country."

The room's occupants moaned and wept as the administrator continued.

"Although we have lost communication with Washington, we have our directives. We will follow the framework that we have all worked with for the last several years. We've planned for this. Each of you know your part. I trust you to implement those directives in as expedient a manner as conceivably possible. Now let's get to work, folks."

He got to his feet.

As the rest of the staff exited the conference room one by one, Response Division Director Gerald Aims sat quietly in his seat until everyone had exited the room. Once everyone was gone, the administrator closed the door.

"All right, Gerry, what do you know?" he asked.

Gerald Aims ran a hand through his salt-and-pepper hair and scratched his head before answering.

"Well, sir, the reality is we are screwed."

Harding scowled.

"But we—"

"I know, I know. We have plans and directives. But we didn't plan for this. My sources in intelligence had been warning about coordinated cyber-attacks to take out our satellites and the electric grid. There were some in the intelligence community who were concerned about information received from sources inside Russia. The source said they had been running large-scale civil defense drills with their citizens in anticipation of retaliatory strikes from the United States and our allies."

"And you think this may be that coordinated attack?"

"What else could it be? The report from the EMP Commission said that most cars and electronics would be unaffected. My folks are saying they were wrong. What we're dealing with here is a super EMP like Dr. Pry predicted."

"What specifically leads you to believe that we have been hit with a super EMP?" Harding asked.

"For starters, more than half the equipment that DOD contractors said would work after an EMP doesn't. Half, Reggie. That means half the trucks needed to take aid to the communities, half of our communications, half of our generators. Anything that was out in the field is gone. The reports I'm receiving are that the only equipment that survived is in the facilities hardened for an 85 kilovolts-per-meter event—and a quarter of those will require repairs before they are operable. None of our facilities were hardened for an a hundred thousand volts-per-meter super EMP attack."

"The generators for this building are working," Harding said.

"Only the ones that weren't plugged into the system. That's why there was a delay before our lights came back on," Aims said.

Aims leaned forward and laid a hand on the binder on the table.

Harding stood and walked over to the window.

After a long pause, Harding turned and said, "I concede that will impact our relief and recovery efforts to the region."

He paused again and turned back to the window.

"But we have orders in place," Harding said. "We have a

national recovery framework. The greatest minds in the country created those plans with all these things in mind. It is our job to do our best to carry out their plans."

Aims turned in his seat to face Harding.

"I understand that we have plans in place. All the career folks will implement that plan to the very best of their abilities. I don't doubt that. But like in our hurricane and other disaster responses, we have too few people with too few resources for the task," Aims said.

"I disagree. We have learned from our mistakes. We have pre-positioned stockpiles of supplies and equipment. We have embedded staff in every major emergency management department in the region," the administrator said.

"Sure, we have pre-positioned supplies and hardened facilities to withstand an EMP. But we never prepared for a super EMP. We can't sustain the entire region for the duration of an emergency of this magnitude on what we have stored."

"We knew that all along. That is why we have prioritized areas."

Director Aims rolled his shoulders and let out a sigh.

"We don't have enough resources to sustain the priority areas for the time that it would take for the recovery division to establish new supply chains. We don't yet know if we will ever be able to reestablish supply chains. The rumors—"

Harding shook his head.

"We knew that as well. That is why executive orders were issued allowing us to seize what we need from distribution centers and other facilities. I know that won't sit well with most folks, but those are the orders we have in place. Understood?"

"Understood," Aims replied.

"Now, let me know when your people have contacted the mayor and chief of police. We need to make sure they understand the emergency orders. Who is Chicago's emergency management director?"

"Ted Sims."

"Oh yeah, I remember him. He's a team player. Have your guys brief him and get to work securing the metro area as soon as possible. I don't want this city erupting into mass chaos on us. That would severely restrict our operations here. You let them know that the federal building and the metro area surrounding it are our highest security priorities at the moment."

"What about the suburbs?"

"Secure the interstates leading to the Joint Field Office facility, as well as the major routes to the state capital. We already have security measures for major infrastructure elements like nuclear power plants, so we will rely on those teams to implement their plans and let us know if they need additional resources. But at this moment, Chicago is our priority. Once we have the city buttoned down, we can move assets to outlying areas as the local authorities need us to," Harding said.

"Reggie, you know most of the smaller county emergency management teams will be understaffed in this situation. Their headquarters will be overrun by day two," Aims said.

"Nothing we can do about that right now. We work our priorities. We will deal with the smaller communities as we have the human resources to do so. Now go find me the mayor," Harding said as he turned and left the room.

Director Aims stood and looked out the sixth-floor window. From his vantage point, the city looked as it always had. The street was crowded with cars and people. The only difference was that very few vehicles were moving. Aims watched a truck attempting to weave in and out of traffic.

"Securing Chicago is going to be a nasty job," Deputy Director Perez said, startling Aims.

Turning to face her, he said, "I hope the police chief is up to the task. He'll have to do what's necessary to maintain order in the city —but at what price? His tactics may only prove to increase tensions with the residents."

Perez nodded.

"I'm glad I'm not the mayor. Having to deal with the city council when a national emergency has made them dispensable would take some finesse," Aims continued.

"Do you think Harding has what it takes to lead this mission?" Perez asked.

"It's a little late for that question now. Whether he has what it takes or not, he's in charge. He'll follow orders and regulations. He's a strict, by-the-book guy."

"What happens when it becomes clear that all our plans and preparations aren't enough for this crisis? Will he do what is necessary then? Or will he stick to the plan and watch what is left of the country fall?"

Perez didn't wait for Aims's reply. She turned and walked out the door.

Aims was loyal to Harding, but even he recognized that Harding's belief that the disaster recovery plan was sufficient to sustain the region for any length of time was not only foolish but dangerous.

Walking over to the conference table, Aims picked up his binder and notepad.

We'll never even get past securing the priority areas.

He sighed and rubbed his temple. He could feel a migraine coming on.

I'm sure glad I picked up my meds this morning.

As Aims walked down the hallway, he could see his staff blocking the door to his office. They were waiting for more details about the attack, and he dreaded having to deliver the news that no one would be leaving the building for the foreseeable future.

Puffing out his cheeks, he let out the breath he held and charged into the group.

His staff erupted in a fury of questions. Aims held up a hand and quieted the room.

"I am sorry to inform you that we don't know the condition of the rest of the country. Dispatches have been sent to the headquarters of the other five states of Region Five. It may be some time before we hear back from them. Right now, our priority is securing and providing relief to Illinois. To do so will require that we all stay here at the federal building until the city is secure. When the authorities tell us that it is safe, we will proceed to Marseilles and set up our offices in the Joint Field Office."

Groans and grumbling came from the unhappy staff.

"As soon as possible, we'll send for your families. In the meantime, we all have jobs to do."

He paused to let the noise die down.

"Now, where are we on logistics?"

CHAPTER 6

Minooka, Illinois
Day of Event

Carl Goff woke up as he did every day, at least the days he slept. He was drenched in sweat, his head pounded, and he vomited until he had nothing left in his stomach. Having not eaten much in the last few days, there wasn't much in there. He'd spent the few dollars he got from pawning a stolen PlayStation on heroin.

Carl looked over to the microwave on the dresser of his motel room. The red light was off. It didn't display the time. He reached up to flip on the lamp. It wasn't working either.

Throwing his legs over the side of the bed, Carl sat up and placed his head in his hands. He rubbed his stubbled chin and tried not to wretch again. Failing, he leaned over and puked into the trash can. Carl removed a cigarette from the pack on the nightstand and lit it. Holding the lighter up, he waved it over his head, scanning the room for the bottle of water he knew he had brought with him the night before.

The door opened, and light flooded the dark room. Carl held a hand over his eyes to ward off the searing pain in his head. He vomited into the trash can again.

"Did you get me anything?" Carl asked over his shoulder.

"I couldn't make it over there," his brother said.

"Why the hell not? Damn it, man. I am dying here. I have to have something, bro."

"The electric went out, and all the cars just died right in the middle of the street. It was the damnedest thing. I was sitting there at the light on 53rd Street, and a big ole pickup truck just barreled through the intersection and slammed right into me. I would have been killed if I hadn't been wearing my seatbelt. Look, it bruised the shit out of me something awful."

"I don't give a shit about your poor little boo-boo. I need my shit, Kelly. I have to have it."

"I don't know what to tell you, bro. The cars ain't working, and I don't know nobody over here with any dope."

Carl reached over and retrieved his cell phone from the nightstand. It was dead. He slammed it on the table with a thud.

"Give me your damn phone," Carl demanded.

"It ain't working either."

"What the fuck is going on here?"

"I don't know. Someone said it was a terrorist attack or some shit. I don't know how they knocked out all the cars and cell phones just by blowing up some buildings or something."

Carl stood, steadying himself on the nightstand. He walked around the bed and across the floor to the window. Peeling back the dingy, smoke-stained curtain, Carl surveyed the scene outside his motel room. Cars were piled up in the intersection down the street. There were more people on foot than Carl had ever seen. He stared out the window for a moment, then closed the curtain. His nausea returned. He walked back to the bed and sat down.

After vomiting into the trash can again, he pulled on his pants.

He put on his long-sleeved, black, button-up shirt, pulled on a dirty hoodie, and slid his feet into an old pair of running shoes. When he reached down the tie his shoes, he remembered he had removed the last lace to use as a tourniquet when he'd shot up the night before.

"I gotta find some H. I can't take this shit, bro."

"I went to Jimmy's. He wasn't home. His old lady said he went up to Chicago and hasn't come back. She said to check with Justin Thayer. He wasn't home either."

"Well, let's go by Jimmy's dad's and see if he left any shit there. Anything will do at this point. I'm bad sick, dude. I need something—anything. I'd take some Xannies or even a blunt, you know, man."

Carl Goff was a thief and a junkie. His whole existence was stealing and buying drugs. He'd been hooked on heroin since he was fourteen, when his mother's boyfriend had first given it to him. Carl and his mother used to shoot up together. At first, she'd shared her stash with Carl—until she disappeared. Neither he nor his brother had seen her in more than six months.

She had gone to turning tricks when the boyfriend supplying her heroin split. Her time away from home became more frequent, and then she didn't come back at all. He had heard that she was working truck stops up and down Interstate 55 between Chicago and St. Louis.

Kelly wanted to file a missing person's report on her. How dumb was that? Like the cops were going to waste their time looking for a junkie whore. Kelly had pouted for two days after Carl had expressed those sentiments, but Carl knew all of it was true. Kelly still held on to the hope that their mom would come home, get clean, and be the mother she had been when he was little. But Carl knew better. Unlike his brother, he had firsthand experience of how impossible it was to kick heroin.

Although most everyone in town knew Jimmy dealt drugs, few knew where he stashed them. Everyone likely thought he kept drugs at his house, but Carl knew Jimmy's old lady would kick his ass if he did. So, six months earlier, Carl had requested a large amount of weed for resale. When Jimmy left his house to get it, Carl had followed him. He hadn't been surprised that Jimmy kept it at his dad's house. Carl and Jimmy used to work on cars there when they were younger. Back then, Jimmy kept his weed in a cigar box in his dad's garage.

Kelly watched the front of the house as Carl went around back. Checking the side door of the detached garage and finding it unlocked, Carl turned the knob and opened the door. Inside was a poppy red 1964 Ford Mustang with its hood up. Along the wall was a workbench lined with greasy tools, empty beer cans, and an ashtray. Carl rushed over to the ashtray.

Carl picked up a roach, pulled a lighter from his pants pocket and lit it. He inhaled the smoke and let out a sigh of relief. The marijuana didn't stop his detox, but it did help relieve the symptoms—especially the nausea.

From a refrigerator near the door, Carl removed a twelve pack of Budweiser, opened one, and downed it. Even though the fridge had stopped running, the beer was still cold. He popped the top on another and took several gulps. Setting the case by the door, Carl returned to the workbench. He rummaged through small storage bins and toolbox drawers.

When he lifted the lid on a large plastic tacklebox, he found what he had been searching for. He pulled out the tray and placed it on the floor. He was just about to reach in and retrieve his prize when he heard his brother talking loudly to someone. Putting the tray back inside the box, he shut the lid and shoved the box back under the bench. He ran over to the beer he had stashed by the door and put it back into the refrigerator. He was tossing the two open cans into the trash when he heard footsteps on the gravel outside the door.

"You better tell that dumb shit brother of yours that he ain't getting no more shit from me until he pays me what he owes. I told him yesterday that he had until tonight to get me my money. World War III or not, he'd better pay me, or he won't have to worry about no North Koreans or Russians or shit. I'll bring down hell on him like he ain't ever seen."

"Don't worry, Jimmy. He'll get you the money. He just needs a little something to get him by today. I got the money," Kelly told the man.

"Bones, go get Kelly a nickel," Jimmy said.

Carl ran around the side of the car and backed into the corner of the garage out of sight of the door as Bones entered the garage and removed the heroin from the tackle box. When Bones left the garage, Carl ran over and took the remaining bags of heroin, Xanax, and marijuana. He left the box where it sat.

Jimmy would think Bones had stolen it.

After hearing the voices fade away down the driveway, Carl left the garage the way he had come in. On his way out, he stuffed two cans of beer into the pocket of his hoodie. After hopping the back fence, Carl ran down a driveway and around the corner to the back of a convenience store.

Sitting beside the dumpster, he placed the beer on the ground next to him. After pulling a syringe, a shoelace, and a lighter from his front pants pocket, Carl removed the heroin from the hoodie. A moment later, warmth flushed over his body. He felt the rush of euphoria as dopamine flooded his brain. Carl leaned back and enjoyed the relief. No more nausea, no more stomach cramps.

Carl awoke behind the store to the sound of glass breaking and loud voices. He rolled a joint and smoked it. He popped two Xanax into his mouth and washed them down with beer. After picking up all his gear and shoving it into his pocket, he pulled a pack of cigarettes from his back pocket. Carl pulled one out with his teeth, lit it, and headed off to the front of the store.

People were running in and out of the broken front doors. Those exiting carried cases of beer, boxes of cigars, and cartons of cigarettes, while others held chips and soda. Some dumb shits had even stolen lottery tickets. Carl wasn't about to get in the middle of that mob.

Two men shoved each other over a case of beer. The parking lot was littered with wrappers and trash. Several of the looters didn't even wait to get their haul home before tearing into it. He considered going in after beer himself, but he didn't feel up to fighting anyone for it.

Most of the fighting was occurring in a cellular service outlet on the opposite corner. Carl stepped back and leaned against the side of the store. Two men knocked down a pregnant woman and took her armful of cell phone cases.

A teenage boy was throwing rocks through the windows of the shop next door. It wasn't long before streams of people were running in and out with armloads of small boxes. He looked up. The sign above the door read Becky's Gifts.

A high-pitched scream from inside the store behind him brought his attention back to the parking lot. A young woman was clutching a man who lay bleeding from his abdomen. People ran around the couple without even looking down.

The woman looked up, pleading. She spotted Carl looking her way.

"Help him. Please!" she cried.

Carl laughed.

"Nobody can help him, lady. He's going to bleed out. Look around. There ain't no cops or ambulances coming to help anyone today."

Carl returned his attention to the door. He might be able to follow someone with beer and jump them for it.

Carl stared at a young girl, probably fifteen or sixteen years old. She was trying to carry four gallons of milk. Her fellow looters pushed and shoved her as she exited. The girl was beautiful. Her long black hair flowed in the wind as she ran across the parking lot—her curves in all the right places. It was then that Carl got the idea of how to get Jimmy's money.

CHAPTER 7

Chicago O'Hare International Airport
Chicago, Illinois
Day of the Event

Travelers had formed a line at the down escalator leading to the baggage claim and ground-level exits. With the power off, people were forced to descend the escalator like a flight of stairs. Many lugged heavy carry-on bags down the steps. Maddie and the Andrews family waited for fifteen minutes for their turn to descend the escalator.

There was no sign of airport security.

As they neared the escalator steps, Rob reached down to take April's bag. April yanked it away and stepped in front of him. Rob rubbed the back of his neck and sighed. April struggled to lift the bulging suitcase into the air as she made her way onto the steps. Rob took Emma's backpack from her as he nudged her gently forward. Maddie stepped onto the escalator right behind Rob. She was pushed from behind by an overweight man, but Rob caught her fall.

"Thanks," Maddie said, before turning to glare at the red-faced brute behind her.

He won't make it five minutes out there.

She chastised herself for making harsh judgments based on his weight, no matter how true she knew it was.

At the bottom of the escalator, a man in a white dress shirt and slacks shoved a woman forward, then he stepped over the woman who sprawled face first onto the tile floor. Others behind him stepped over the woman as well and rushed toward the exit doors. Finally, an older woman stopped and took the lady's arm to help her up. She too was shoved to the ground. Now two women lay in a heap at the bottom of the escalator. A teenage boy put both hands on the escalator rails and hopped over the two women. He shoved an older man out of the way before rushing toward the exit.

A tall man in a sports jersey hopped over the two women. He turned and grabbed them by the arms and pulled the pair away from the bottom of the escalator. The man was helping the older woman to her feet when Rob stepped around them. Those leaving the escalator barely glanced at the trio in their rush to hit the exit. Maddie looked back after she passed them. The man was helping the women pick up their belongings from floor when another large man plowed into them, knocking them all back to the ground.

No good deed goes unpunished.

At the exit doors, glass littered the floor and sidewalk. The glass of the door had been broken and everyone was stepping through the empty frame of the locked door. As passengers grew impatient waiting their turn, Maddie could hear more glass breaking and saw groups of people splitting off toward the new exit.

After exiting the airport, the four of them followed the crowd. Everyone headed for the main street leading south and away from the terminal. Maddie looked over her shoulder. Smoke rose over the top of the terminal, and the putrid kerosene smell of burning jet fuel filled the air. A man in tattered, bloody clothes wandered aimlessly in the parking lot.

When they reached the street, Maddie looked up. The sign read Mannheim Road. After crossing the road in the crosswalk, they headed south. The sidewalk was filled with people fleeing the airport mixed with the stranded motorists who had given up on their vehicles. People walked out into the congested four-lane street lined with abandoned cars.

Maddie could hear an occasional car engine and distant sirens. The traffic signal lights were dark. Bloody passengers sat in their vehicles with the doors propped open. April stepped in front of Emma to shield the girl's view of the gory scenes.

April continued to struggle with her suitcase. Whenever they could pick up speed, the case would teeter back and forth on its wheels before crashing sideways. The last time it had fallen, April had bent over to pick it up and someone behind her had tripped over her, sending her to the ground. Glaring at Rob, April rubbed her bloody palms on her jeans. She picked up the sandal that had flown off her foot in the fall. Placing her hand on Rob's shoulder, April strapped the shoe back onto her foot. She huffed and pulled down the bottom of her tank top. She looked over her shoulder at Maddie and scowled. It was all Maddie could do not to roll her eyes at the woman.

Does she somehow think I was responsible for her fall?

Maddie sure hoped the woman had a suitcase full of food or other survival gear, because her expensive clothes and jewelry wouldn't keep her family alive. What it could do, however, was get them killed, especially if they ran into someone who wanted to steal what was in that bag.

Maddie thought about how her dad would have handled the situation. She knew one thing for sure—that bag would have stayed at the airport. Her dad would have ditched the Andrews family as soon as he saw how stubborn April was being. But he had the training and skills to make it alone. Maddie didn't have those skills—not enough for this situation, anyway, she thought. She'd have to bite her tongue and hope for the best.

The crowd walked across the overpass spanning a large rail-yard. To the west were rows and rows of boxcars sitting on the tracks waiting for trains that might never come.

I bet there's a lot of food in those cars.

Looters had already broken into the steel shipping containers and were carting large boxes across the tracks and heading east walking on the railbed. Commercial buildings and shops lined the street beyond the railyard. On one corner was a convenience store. A large crowd had gathered in the parking lot. Men loitered there, leaning on cars, watching each pedestrian like lions eyeing their prey.

Maddie wanted to cross over to the other side when she saw them. Rob put his arm around Emma and led them to the middle of the street. They made their way around one stranded vehicle after another, finally passing the convenience store.

As they passed a fried chicken restaurant, Maddie's stomach growled. She looked at her watch. Her dad had given it to her for her thirteenth birthday. For most people, ever-present cell phones had replaced watches. While her friends wore their Fitbits and Apple watches, Maddie had held on to her G-Shock self-winding watch.

She hadn't remembered to fuel up until now. Her last meal had been that morning at her grandmother's house. Her mom had made sausage and pancakes, Maddie's favorite. Maddie had stayed three days in San Diego to help her mother care for Grand. Maddie knew Grand wouldn't be around much longer and wondered how her grandfather would get along without his wife. Although Maddie loved her grandfather, she had thought him incapable of caring for himself even before his stroke. Beth said Grandpa Frank only pretended to be helpless. Maddie was not convinced. If his help-lessness was all an act, he gave an Oscar-worthy performance. Grand had always hovered and controlled Grandpa Frank. It was part of their relationship and seemed to work for them. Her grand-parents had been happily married for over twenty years.

Maddie had had exams she couldn't miss, so she had scheduled a flight back to Ohio. When the time came for Maddie to return to college, she had felt terrible about leaving her mother to deal with everything by herself—but she was still relieved to go. Why her stepdad couldn't close his dental practice for one lousy week to be with his wife, Maddie couldn't understand. He likely would have done so, though, if her mom had asked. Since she hadn't, she must have wanted to do it all alone. Maybe her mom thought it would be easier not to have to deal with other people in the way. Maddie didn't know if that was true. In the end, Maddie had been glad to be on her way back to Kent State and her boyfriend, Lane.

Maddie and the Andrews family were still walking in the middle of the street, but the main crowd remained on the sidewalk. The group from the airport had thinned out, from what Maddie could tell. Either that or, unlike April, they had given up the struggle with their heavy carry-on bags.

Maddie craned her neck around to see if anyone was watching her. She knew she'd need to stay fueled up from here on out if she was going to make it the three hundred miles home.

Not trying to be obvious, Maddie slowly reached into the stretch pocket on the front of her pack and pulled out a Clif Bar. She had pre-torn all the wrappers in that pocket—a habit formed from many frustrating attempts to rip open packets while on long endurance runs. Another runner had given her that tip, and it had worked well for her.

Shoving half the bar into her mouth, Maddie looked around again. She chewed as she walked, keeping her head on a swivel, knowing that people would be hungry enough to take her food from her soon. She could not let that happen.

A large group stood in the intersection ahead. Maddie shot Rob a quizzical look. As they passed, she saw that most of them held signs.

"They're protesting?" Maddie asked, leaning toward Rob.

One tall, African American man held a sign that read, "Enough is Enough." Maddie stepped over a sign on the sidewalk that read, "Time for the Mayor to Go."

The large group seemed confused as to what had happened.

Rob put an arm around Emma and held her close as they passed through the crowd. April picked up her bag. They moved quickly down the street away from the action, not slowing their pace until they could no longer see them. April was limping. No doubt she was getting huge blisters from wearing sandals better suited for a day at the beach than a fifty-mile hike through the city streets of Chicago.

I bet she wished she'd packed tennis shoes.

At least Emma was wearing tennis shoes, although she was limping as well. They hadn't even walked three miles and her companions were showing definite signs of wear and tear. The blood had stopped dripping from April's hands. They were dirty and likely had tiny bits of gravel and sand in the cuts. She considered whether she should offer to clean and bandage it for her.

Maddie was not carrying much in the way of medical supplies —she usually didn't. She had antibiotic ointment and Band-Aids, but that was about it. When she ran, there were always doctors and nurses at the first aid tents at the aid stations, so she had stopped carrying more than that.

They walked in silence for another two or three miles. There appeared to be less looting the farther they walked from the airport. They passed over another railyard, not as large as the one by the airport. There were maybe a hundred railcars on the tracks. All the food and other products would go undelivered, even if the trains were still running. If the big rigs that hauled the products to stores were operational, they would be stuck in the traffic jams.

Emma pointed to a group of people jumping down from one of the railcars closest to the street. A woman reached up and grabbed the small children being lowered to her. There appeared to be six or seven of them. None could have been more than five years old.

Rob said something to Emma that Maddie couldn't hear, then took her hand, guiding her along faster. Maddie was not sure what that was about, but it was apparent to her that Rob shared her idea that they needed to get away from the railyard and its looters.

A few blocks later, they came to an intersection. Emma reached over and pulled on the bottom of Maddie's pack. Maddie's first thought was that she was trying to take something from her. She turned and Emma pointed up to the street sign.

"Madison Street," Emma said, a broad smile on her face.

Emma had said little the entire time they'd been together. The events at the airport no doubt had traumatized the young girl. Maddie smiled and nodded.

"My castle is just down there," Maddie said with a chuckle.

Emma laughed, then returned to her mother's side, her spiraled red curls bouncing with each step.

April's face was expressionless, her shoulders slumped, and her head hung low. Her limp had become more pronounced. Maddie had experienced terrible blisters before she'd learned how to buy properly fitted shoes. April had developed a rhythm with her suitcase, and it flopped around less. Maddie felt sorry for the woman —some, anyway.

Her feet aren't the only thing that will hurt like hell before she gets home. Her arms will be toast long before then.

After a few more miles, the crowds and traffic jams were thinning out, but there was still a lot of people out on the streets. Rob tapped Maddie on the shoulder.

"I think we should find a safe place to stop and rest for the night. The sun is setting behind the buildings, and it'll be dark soon."

Maddie didn't want to stop. Her goal had been—and still was —to get as far away from the city as possible. The presence of protestors had promoted memories of the protests-turned-riots in

St. Louis. Streets had been blocked and stores looted and burned. The police had been powerless to stop it. She did not want to be in the city when all that started.

They had made it ten miles, at most. She could have made that in an hour on her own. Although she could travel faster without them, she doubted that it would be safer.

"All right," Maddie said, turning her head and scanning for a safe place to stop.

Rob pointed to an alley between a garage door repair shop and a drycleaners. Maddie nodded in acknowledgment, and they slipped between the buildings.

Behind the shop was a row of small storage sheds. Someone had broken the locks and the doors stood open. The contents of the sheds lay scattered on the asphalt parking lot. Rob pushed aside boxes and began to go inside.

"Rob, no. If we go in and shut the door, the next person looking to loot them might find us," Maddie said.

Maddie pointed to the space between the sheds. Behind the row of sheds was a narrow strip of grass. In the dark, the sheds would hide them from passersby.

Maddie sat cross-legged on the grass and drank from her wrist flask. Rob removed a twenty-ounce bottle of Diet Coke from his backpack and handed it to Emma. April flopped down onto the grass and removed her sandals. She removed a bottle of water from her tote bag and poured the liquid onto her mangled feet.

Maddie winced when she saw them. She knew all too well how that felt. Her feet still ached a little from her last one-hundred-mile race. Injuries like that sidelined a lot of dedicated runners. The condition of April's feet was slowing them all down.

How long before she can go no farther?

Maddie removed the first aid kit from a side zipper pocket and slid over to where April was sitting.

"I have Band-Aids."

Tears formed in April's eyes. Maddie removed a water flask from her pack and squirted the liquid onto April's other foot.

"Do you have something you could use to dry your feet?"

She nodded and reached over to unzip her suitcase. She winced in pain. April unzipped the bag and threw back the flap to reveal a stack of neatly packed clothes in airtight space bags. April lifted a bag out of the case, exposing a pair of white tennis shoes. She lifted the shoes in the air and shook her head.

"I can't believe I forgot I brought these."

Maddie's gaze was on the copper urn wrapped in plastic. Maddie's eyes widened, and she turned to April. Tears now streamed down the woman's sweaty face. Her gaze went from the urn back to Maddie.

"You must think me stubborn and petty for holding on to my bag in all this chaos," she said, sniffling.

"No," Maddie lied.

Rob came over and stood beside his wife. He placed a hand on her shoulder, tears filling his eyes. April returned her gaze to Maddie, let out a sigh, and picked up the urn.

"I just couldn't leave it. It is all I have left of my son," April said, caressing the urn in her arms.

"We were headed to the beach in Florida to spread some of his ashes. He loved the beach," Rob said. "He wanted to use his Make-a-Wish on a family trip to the beach, but—" Rob stopped and looked away.

"The Cubbies came to his party instead. He was happy, but I really wanted to go to the beach. I hate baseball," Emma said, taking her father's hand.

"I'm so sorry," Maddie choked out, fighting tears of her own.

She felt so bad for them. Maddie had lost her father—and that was awful—but she couldn't imagine how hard losing a child would be.

"How old was—"

A loud crash sounded behind them. They all turned.

The sound had come from the back of the shops. Maddie heard a whoosh, then a light pierced the darkness.

Maddie peaked out from around the side of the shed.

Fire. They've started burning down the city already.

"The building is on fire," Maddie whispered over her shoulder.

"I think we will still be safe here. We should be far enough away that the sheds don't catch fire," Rob said.

"I hope so. There's a huge crowd out there," Maddie said, scooting back away from the corner of the shed.

Rob reached over and wrapped his arms around Emma, pulling her close. She laid her head in his lap, her curls spilling onto the grass. She was asleep in minutes. Maddie wished she could sleep like that. She hadn't slept well the last few years, often lying awake half the night rattled by every little noise. Her mother had a security system installed, but it did little to stop the nightmares.

No one spoke as they listened to the sounds of breaking glass and the yelling of the growing crowds. There were no sirens. The police were not coming in their riot gear to dispel the mobs with tear gas. Even if they did, there wouldn't be enough officers to quell the violence and looting that would occur that night and over the next few days. It wouldn't take long before there was little left to loot or burn.

That is when the gangs will turn savage.

Maddie couldn't allay the sense of urgency to get out of the city. Everything in her said...

Run.

CHAPTER 8

Dixon Garage Door Repair Shop
Bellwood, Illinois
Event + 1 day

Rob had proposed they take two-hour watches. They would take turns sleeping. When Maddie's watch was up, she didn't bother waking Rob. The odor of the burning buildings and the screams that pierced the night made sure she wouldn't sleep.

The crowds began breaking up as dawn approached. Maddie imagined they'd go home and sleep through the day to rest up for the next night's riots and looting. Maddie intended to not be in the city to find out if she was correct.

Emma squirmed in her dad's lap before opening her eyes. Smiling down at her, he wiped wayward strands of hair from her face.

April and Emma were seated cross-legged on the ground next to Rob. Maddie was struck by how much Emma looked like April. Emma, with her long curly red hair and green eyes, looked like a younger version of her mother. Both were slender and petite. Maddie favored her mom and had received similar comments when she was younger. She found it irritating to be compared to her mother.

April retrieved a brush from her tote bag and began brushing Emma's hair.

"Just hold still, Em, and I'll get done a whole lot faster," April said.

"I hate my hair."

"I think it is beautiful, Emma. It looks like—"

"Don't say it!" Rob and April said in unison.

They looked at each other and laughed.

"I was going to say that I love your curls," Maddie said.

"Well, I hate them," Emma grumbled.

"She gets teased by the boys at school. They call her Princess Merida," April whispered.

"I hate Merida," Emma pouted.

"I know, Em. You're so much prettier and smarter," Rob said, holding her down and tickling her belly.

Another crashing sound brought them back to reality. Maddie stood and looked around the side of the sheds but didn't see anyone in the immediate vicinity.

Returning to her spot on the grass, Maddie retrieved a Mayday bar from a side pouch. She checked the level of the water left in her water bladder.

Half full.

She still had enough food and water to get out of the city. She wondered if the Andrews family had any water left. She doubted they were carrying any food.

April and Rob leaned in close and whispered. Maddie couldn't make out what the Andrews were discussing, but she could guess at the topic. They had no food or water.

Maddie reached into her pack and took out three energy bars

and removed a water flask. She leaned over and handed them to April.

April looked up. She hesitated, looked over to Emma, then took them from Maddie.

"Thank you," Rob said, reaching over and taking one from April.

Tearing the package open, Rob handed the energy bar to Emma before taking one for himself. April took a sip of water then gave the flask to Emma.

"I don't have much left. We'll need to find food and water before we leave the city, I'm afraid," Maddie said.

Rob appeared to think it over, then nodded. They would have to join the looting. Maddie considered the moral dilemma of stealing. She hated thieves, but it could mean the difference between making it out of the city alive and not. She hoped the store owners would understand, considering the circumstances.

Maddie and the Andrews gathered their bags and packs. After inching her way out from between the storage sheds, Maddie stood and scanned the area. The parking lot was empty. The roof of the brick building was totally burned out. Black char marks stained the brick facades.

Stepping from the corner of the shed, Maddie spotted a teenage boy sitting in a parked car at the end of the alley. Seconds later, a large group of boys ran down the alley and circled the vehicle, trapping the boy inside. Someone in the group slammed a brick through the driver's side window while another tried to get the door open. The teen behind the wheel slapped at the hands reaching into the car. The tallest of the boys seized hold of the boy's collar and began dragging him through the shattered window.

Letting go of Emma's hand, Rob yelled, "Stay here," as he sprinted toward the car. April and Emma called after him, but he kept going. When he reached the group of boys, he shouted for them to stop. The older of the boys spun around, lunged forward, and smashed Rob in the face with a brick from the burned-out building. The force knocked Rob back and he fell hard, hitting his head on the concrete.

"Rob!" April screamed.

April raced toward Rob. The mob of boys grabbed her. They pounced on her in unison, knocking her to the ground. Each thug pounded and kicked her over and over. Emma stood frozen.

"No!" Emma wailed.

As Emma's foot lifted from the pavement, Maddie seized her by the shirt, nearly jerking her off her feet. Wrapping her other arm around the girl's midsection, Maddie turned Emma away from the bloody scene.

Maddie looked over her shoulder. The tallest boy drew out a pistol and pressed it to the passenger's head. The sound of the shot startled the other boys. As the gang turned their attention toward the car, Maddie took Emma by the hand, pulling her from the alley and away from the slaughter of her parents.

"Let me go! I have to help them!" Emma cried as she clawed at Maddie's hand.

Maddie stopped running but didn't release the girl. Emma yanked as hard as she could to get away, but Maddie held tight.

"Emma," Maddie said, placing one hand on the girl's shoulder. Bending down, Maddie placed her forehead against Emma's.

"You can't save them. Those boys have guns. There's nothing we can do for them. They would want you to run away. They would want you to live."

As Maddie wrapped her arms around her, Emma sobbed into Maddie's shoulder.

Maddie held Emma tight as she surveyed the street. The sun was beginning to rise, and she got her first glimpse of the damage done during the night. Maddie took Emma by the shoulders and looked her in the eyes. Wiping tears from the girl's face, Maddie said, "Emma, things are bad here in the city, and it is going to get worse when it gets dark. We have to go. We have to run as fast as we can and get as far from the city as possible."

Emma looked up and over her shoulder. She nodded.

After wiping her nose on her sleeve, Emma took a deep breath. "You ready?"

"Yes," Emma said, her voice still quivering.

The two girls ran for their lives.

They ran between stalled cars and around the hordes of people blocking the sidewalks. Maddie wanted to put as much distance as she could between them and the crowded city, but it was slow going. It was harder than the start of a marathon. At least with a marathon, runners eventually spread out and she could break away from the pack. Here, people were slowly walking along or just loitering on the sidewalks.

Although she tried running in the middle of the road, the numerous stalled and wrecked vehicles made even that strategy fruitless. After sidestepping a family walking four abreast on the sidewalk, they wound their way through a maze of cars blocking an intersection. Stepping back onto the side, she heard a group of young men catcalling her from the door of the shop behind them.

"Hey, baby, why don't you come over here, and we can go party?"

"Yeah, we'd love to show you a good time," said a man wearing a large gold chain around his neck and baggy jeans hanging below his butt.

Maddie looked down. Emma looked up impassively. Maddie looked back at the men. She wasn't too worried about the baggy jeans guy. If he tried to chase her, he would no doubt trip as his baggy pants fell around his ankles. She had seen that happen many times on the police shows. Live PD was one of her favorites. She thought her mom secretly had a crush on the officer from the Tulsa Gang Unit. She had to admit he was cute, for an old guy. Much better looking than her stepdad.

A crowd had gathered at the next corner, blocking the sidewalk and southbound lanes of traffic. When Maddie got close, she and Emma crossed over and ran south in the northbound lane. Although she gave it all her little ten-year-old legs could handle, Emma was beginning to tire. It was taking Maddie more effort to pull her along, but she didn't dare release the girl's hand. She'd likely slow and be swallowed by the crowd.

As they approached the intersection, Maddie could see what had drawn the group. Two men were on the ground playing tug-of-war with a case of beer—no doubt looted from the liquor store on the corner.

Slowing, Maddie stared at the fight as they passed them. Feeling a tug on her backpack, she swung around. One of the men who had been catcalling her had grabbed her. Luckily, he didn't have a firm grasp. As she turned, he lost his grip. She shoved him and he fell backward.

"Back off, creeper," Maddie yelled.

Maddie grabbed Emma by the arm and shuffled through the throng of people. Immediately after they emerged from the crowd, they took off running as fast as Emma could go.

Maddie took a chance and looked over her shoulder, just as Emma tripped over a trash can in the middle of the sidewalk and tumbled to the ground. Quickly grabbing her up, Maddie took off again, but the delay was enough for two other men to gain on the girls.

Maddie and Emma ran around a group of people on the sidewalk, jumped the curb, and ran across a four-lane street. Maddie looked behind her as she rounded the corner of a shop. She no longer saw the men.

Behind the store was a long parking lot that spanned the length of a row of shops. A tall, wooden privacy fence separated the stores from the apartment building behind it. In the back of the lot, pushed up next to the fence, sat two large, green dumpsters. Maddie shoved Emma behind them and then slid in beside her. Emma scooted back and sat in the corner with her back against the wooden fence. The space was cramped, and her knees touched her chest.

"I saw them run back here," a male voice said.

"Well, they ain't here now."

"They have to be here somewhere. I doubt that little one could jump the fence. Check the back doors. Maybe they went inside."

Maddie heard the doors rattle and then a thud. They had kicked the door. She peeked out from between the two dumpsters. The two men were still searching the parking lot.

From her place in the corner, she could see along the length of the fence and part of the side street. The men paced. As they approached the end of the building farthest from her, Maddie let out the breath she had been holding. The men stopped at the driveway entrance on the side street. Staring at something in the distance, the taller of the two put his arm out, pushing his companion back into the parking lot. The two men pressed their shoulders into the wooden fence. The taller one peered around the end post toward whatever had caught their interest.

Since the men were distracted, Maddie seized the chance to slip out from behind the dumpster. She tugged on Emma's arm, but the girl refused to budge. Maddie crawled to the end of the last dumpster and waved for Emma to join her. Shaking her head, Emma whimpered, burying her face in her knees.

Maddie slid back in to rouse the girl. Emma moaned. Maddie turned to see if the men had heard her. She sat down next to Emma and placed an arm around her.

Maddie looked around the back of the dumpster and saw the taller man jump out in front of a young woman. The second man stepped behind her. The tallest creeper grabbed the girl's right arm and began dragging her into the parking lot. The girl screamed and kicked the man in the groin. He let go of her arm, and the girl was able to take a few steps before the second man grabbed her by her long ponytail.

Yanking back on her long locks, the man pulled her off balance and she fell to the ground. He dragged her by her hair into a grassy area along the fence. The second man, having recovered enough to stand, reared back and kicked the girl in the ribs, causing her to double over and scream in pain.

The men tore at the girl's clothes. Maddie sat frozen in place. Her heart pounded in her chest. She wanted to do something— anything. She needed to rescue this helpless girl, but she knew she couldn't overpower two strong men.

She pressed her back against the dumpster. There was nothing she could do.

If only I had my rifle. Or my knife or pepper spray or something. Anything.

She placed her hands over her ears. She couldn't stand to listen to the two men's grunts. Her mind went blank. Time just stopped.

She recalled the camping trip she had taken with her family to Cuivre River State Park when she was ten years old. She and her brother Zach had played hide-and-seek in the bushes along the campsite while their parents prepared dinner over the campfire. Zach startled her and she shot up, catching her hair in the brambles. It had taken her mother ten long, agonizing minutes to untangle her long hair from the bush. Her dad had merely walked over, unsheathed his knife, and cut the branches. Maddie thought he had cut her hair.

After her mother removed the final strands from the grip of the stickers, her father said, "That is why you should always wear your hair up—and in a hat—when you're out here. Just imagine if it had been a bad guy who had a hold of your hair and won't let go."

Picturing the girl being dragged by her hair, Maddie reached up and felt the top of her head. Her hair was still in its tight bun. Any loose strands were tucked under her headband just the way she always wore it. She hoped it was sufficient for the apocalypse.

Gazing over to Emma's long hair, Maddie took two hair ties from her pack. She gently wrapped Emma's hair into a ponytail. She twirled it around her hand, wrapping it into a bun before slipping a tie around it. Giving it a gentle tug, Maddie secured the second tie. She poked wayward curls into the bun. Emma looked up at Maddie, her eyes full of tears. Maddie embraced her, rocking her side to side.

~

The girl's screams had stopped. Maddie no longer heard the men talking. She checked her watch. It was nearly five o'clock. They had been sitting behind the dumpsters for hours. There was only about an hour before the sun went down and the real crazies came out to play. At least that was what her father said would happen, and his predictions had been dead-on so far.

After sliding to the end, Maddie peeked out from behind the dumpster.

Maddie gasped. She placed a hand over her mouth to stifle her sobs as she looked where the young woman lay, naked and bloody.

Finally regaining her composure, Maddie looked for the two men. Not seeing or hearing them, she inched out of her hiding place and stood. She waved for Emma to follow. This time, Emma complied.

Maddie sucked in a breath at the sight of all the blood. She took a step forward, intending to help the girl, but there was so much blood, the girl was most likely dead or soon would be. She took tentative steps over to the young woman, bent down, and wiped a strand of hair from her eyes.

"I'm so sorry that I couldn't help you," Maddie said, removing a bandana from her side pouch and placing it over the girl's naked midsection.

A loud crash and the sound of breaking glass startled her. It had only been twenty-four hours and people were this violent. As more and more people figured out that they could do anything without fear of prison, Maddie knew it would become increasingly more dangerous to be on the streets. She needed a new route—one away from the commercial district and the looters.

Maddie looked up and down the side street. She couldn't be sure where the girl's killers had gone, but it was time to go. She needed to get Emma away from the city. Emma was her responsibility now, and she was not going to let her down.

CHAPTER 9

FEMA Headquarters
Federal Building
Chicago, Illinois
Event + 1 day

After spending the night on the lumpy sofa in his office, Director Aims opened his eyes and stared at the ceiling. He had just drifted off to sleep when a knock on his door stirred him.

"Come in," Aims barked.

The red-faced courier handed Director Aims an envelope and rushed back out of the office. Aims focused on the envelope and managed to rip the top flap open in a few seconds. He reached in and pulled out a handwritten report.

The Surge Capacity Force members are currently being inserted into the Rapid Response teams. The Illinois National Guard has mobilized to their assigned coordinates and has already begun securing the points of entry to the city. The Chicago Emergency Management reports that their officers encountered resistance from several large groups which appear to be part of protests in progress before the EMP. Those groups are now stranded near the airport. Passengers from O'Hare International have flooded the streets.

After a night of looting and rioting, many businesses near the airport are on fire. The Stone Park police station was set on fire as well. The police departments have begun moving the crowds off the streets in that area block by block. The immediate area surrounding your facility on Clark Street has been secured.

As the Guard troops encounter people trying to enter the city, they have been directing them to the Disaster Recovery Centers at the church in Manteno. The DRCs have opened all but nine of the pre-positioned centers around the city. As soon as sufficient personnel to operate those centers have been located, they will be operational as well.

Incident Management teams and Logistics have implemented their orders. However, just like the recovery centers, locating staff members has proven more challenging than anticipated. With the lack of satellite communications, teams have been forced to go to each office to pick up personnel and transport them to work. This has put a strain on our transportation capabilities, but we anticipate a ninety percent solution once workers are transported to their duty stations. everything will run as planned.

Illinois Emergency Management (IEMA) has requested additional transportation support to facilitate movement of Emergency Support Function Six NGO and Red Cross volunteers.

William Krauss,
Logistics Manager,
FEMA

Aims folded the memo and placed it on his desk. After pulling a notepad from his desk drawer, he removed a pen from his shirt pocket. He sighed. Life without computers and cell phones made mundane tasks a chore. What used to take seconds now took hours. His handwritten orders had to be given to couriers who would hand-deliver them to his teams in the field.

He took a deep breath and wrote his response.

Keep me updated on Chicago PD's progress. Go ahead and provide IEMA with available transportation after major objectives have been met and priority locations are secured. I want a status report on the number of Guard troops and disaster agency volunteers that are unaccounted for as soon as a roster can be made.

After struggling to slide the memo into an interoffice manila envelope, Aims stood and opened his door. He motioned for his secretary and held out the envelope.

"The administrator just sent word that he wants to see you in his office in twenty minutes," the woman said.

"Any word from Washington?" he asked.

"Not that I am aware of, sir."

Aims stretched and rolled his shoulders. He walked down the hall and entered the men's room. Looking at himself in the mirror, he noticed the dark circles under his eyes. After washing his face, he tucked in his shirt and straightened his tie. Running a finger over his teeth, he lamented that he didn't keep an overnight kit in his desk anymore. He hadn't needed it since his promotion to director.

Administrator Harding didn't look like he'd slept any better than Aims had, even though he also had a sofa in his office. Aims looked over at the papers strewn about the floor and covering the sofa cushions. It confirmed his suspicion that the administrator hadn't slept either.

"What do you have to report on securing the city?" Harding asked, looking up from the mound of papers on his desk.

He stood up and poured a glass of water, handing it to Aims.

After taking a sip, Aims gave him a summary of the situation report he had received from Krauss. When he finished, Harding said nothing. An awkward silence hung between them. Aims debated if he should ask Harding if he had heard anything from Washington or the other regions, but Harding was deep in thought

Breaking the silence, Harding said, "We've been unable to

communicate with Washington. There are rumors that D.C. was hit directly by one of the missiles. It is only an unconfirmed report at the moment, so keep that to yourself. I've sent word to Indiana to dispatch a team to D.C. to confirm the status of the capital and secure any new orders from the White House. Until then, we continue operating under the emergency orders."

Harding leaned forward and placed his elbows on his desk. He ran his hand across his stubbled face. Although his skin complexion obscured any dark circles, Aims could still see prominent bags forming under Harding's brown eyes.

"My staff is anxious to get moved out of the city. As you can imagine, they are concerned for their families," Aims said.

"I'm sure they are, but we have a crisis to handle here. We'll move as soon as we get the all-clear from the security teams," Harding said.

Aims said nothing.

Harding was quiet a moment before clearing his throat. He stood and pulled a binder from the shelf beside his desk. The EMP had turned the clock back to the 1800s. Paper copies were all they had to go by now. He placed the binder on the desk and opened it. He thumbed through tabs until he found the section he'd been searching for. With an index finger, he pointed to the heading at the top of the page.

"If we receive news that D.C. is gone, we're required to implement the continuity and recovery plans."

Harding's expression was grim. The binder held the continuity plan that no one ever wanted to have to implement. The one that meant the cavalry was never coming to the rescue, that they were on their own and soon the streets would resemble the wild, wild west.

"That would make you the head of the region. How do you think the governors are going to react?" Aims asked.

"Some will resist while others will be relieved to have someone to blame when their residents start complaining about the slow recovery."

Aims locked eyes with Harding.

"Slow recovery. That is an understatement, don't you think?"

Harding puffed out his cheeks and let out a lungful of air. Placing his hands in his pockets, he looked down at his shoes. His business casual and tasseled loafers were entirely inappropriate for the apocalypse

"Sir, you and I both know that there's no recovering from this disaster."

Harding held up a hand.

"We have a plan, Gerry. The plan is a recovery plan. It is not our job to do nation-building. We don't get to decide what communities live and which ones have to fend for themselves. We live in the United States of America. The United States."

Harding's face was hard. This time, Harding was the initiator as their eyes locked.

Aims broke eye contact and looked toward the window. He imagined all the resources that were being wasted at that moment. Poorly protected recovery centers would soon be overrun with people looking for assistance. Resources would soon run out, and those people would not have the skills or ability to care for themselves in the new world.

"Let's wait two days," Harding said. "If we don't hear back from Indiana or if we hear that D.C. has fallen, we will begin President Rhynard's continuity plan."

Harding closed the binder and placed it back on the shelf.

"And at what point will you decide that it is time to implement General Garland's continuity plan?" Aims asked.

Harding spun around and faced Aims with fury all over his face.

"Never!" Harding said, veins bulging in his forehead.

Harding's eyes were almost black. Aims tilted his head and studied the man's hard features. He didn't doubt that Harding meant what he said. No matter how dire the situation got, Harding would not sacrifice the many to save the few, even if that meant that they all perished.

In the early days of Rhynard's presidency, General Garland had laid out the plan to the president and his cabinet as a remote possibility scenario for planning purposes only. No one in the cabinet had taken it seriously. It had been one of several dozen proposals put forth in the planning stages of the new president's framework for a recovery plan. Aims would likely have never even known about it had he not been sleeping with someone with contacts in the cabinet. She and the others had laughed it off as lunacy. But it made perfect sense to Aims, especially in a scenario like the one playing out in the country at that precise moment.

Did Harding think the Russians, Chinese, and Iranians had launched the attacks only to sideline the United States?

Aims held eye contact with Harding as he took his seat.

"I know we discussed his plan in jest. I was just joking. Nothing to get so worked up about. We've planned for as many scenarios as possible, and we are a resilient nation, after all. I'm sure—with your leadership—Region Five will not only recover, but it'll also thrive," Aims said, doing his best to wear a genuine smile.

Harding's shoulders relaxed. As he took his seat, he drew in a deep breath and let it out, making a braying noise.

"What I don't need right now, Aims, is an ass-kisser. But in case there is a thread of sincerity in that statement, I thank you."

A knock on the door broke the tension. Harding turned toward the door and said, "Yes, come in."

A National Guard soldier poked his head around the door.

"Administrator Harding, we have cleared the route to Marseilles and transport units should be here to move you and your staff later this afternoon."

"Excellent. We will be ready."

Harding turned to Aims.

"Make sure everyone is ready. Let me know if anyone gives you any problems. We can't have staff thinking they are exempt."

Aims rose to his feet and walked over to the door. With his hand on the knob, he turned back and looked over his shoulder.

"I don't think anyone will have a problem loading up for the trip. It is their reactions when they get there that we'll have to handle."

Harding looked up from the papers on his desk.

He stared at Aims.

"Do you anticipate having problems when we get there?" he asked.

Aims furrowed his brow, unsure what to answer.

"Well, they likely won't be happy when they discover that not all their families have been brought there."

Harding let out a heavy sigh and rubbed his forehead.

"I told the director we should have made it clear which essential staff would be allowed accompanied duty and which won't," Harding confessed. "When we arrive, they won't be told their families can't join them. They will only be told that they will join them when transportation is available. That should hold them off until the buses start arriving with refugees," Harding said.

"Maybe by then it won't matter. Security will have been established and any personnel issues can be handled by the continuity teams. We will have more staff than we know what to do with at that point. So, if we lose some, it won't really matter," Aims said.

"That's what I was thinking as well. Just make sure we don't lose anyone on your team. They are all vital to what we will need to set up in Marseilles."

"I'll take care of that," Aims said, turning the knob.

He looked over Harding's office one last time. He imagined they were all about to face the harsh reality of life outside their air-conditioned, sixth-floor offices. Closing the door behind him, he inhaled deeply.

I so need a nap or a drink or both.

CHAPTER 10

Morris, Illinois
   Event, + 1 day

"Where the hell you been, Kelly? I've been waiting here for hours," said Carl.

"I was looking for you. I hung around Jimmy's place for a long time. When Jimmy and Pickle left, I went into the garage to find you, and that's how I knew you'd had left."

"That don't matter none now. Where's my shit?"

Kelly handed Carl the bags and flopped into the ripped upholstered chair by the window of Carl's motel room.

"What the hell do you think you're doing? This ain't no time to sit and chill. We have to get Jimmy his money. That ain't gonna happen sitting in this shithole all day. So, get your ass up and let's go."

Carl was obscured by an illuminated bank of smoke when he opened the door.

"How we gonna get him money? I went by the pawnshop on Third Street on my way back here, and it was on fire. There was a crowd of people throwing Molotov cocktails in all the windows on that block."

Carl stopped in the doorway, turned, and punched the door.

He hadn't considered that pawnshops would be the first places looted. And then, everyone would have shit to sell that'd make his shit worthless.

He shut the door, walked over to the bed, and sat down, placing his head in his hands. The scene at the convenience store played over and over in his mind. He knew there must be something he could boost that'd still be worth money, enough money to pay Jimmy back and keep him in dope until this shit passed.

Think, Carl. Think.

As he replayed the scene again, he remembered the girl. She was out there, alone—his for the taking. He knew a guy, someone who dealt in high-end stuff like that. He needed to find him and see what he'd pay for something of that quality. He doubted he could find that exact girl again, but there would be plenty of other fruit for the picking.

"Let's go find Vance Haven," said Carl, disappearing into the whirls of smoke at the door. He dragged Kelly out, nearly causing him to trip over his own feet.

"What the hell do we want with Haven? He's a scumbag pimp. He ain't gonna give you no money."

Carl knew Kelly hated the man. Haven was the guy who hooked their mom up with the biggest mover of lot lizards in this part of the country. Kelly didn't understand what it was like for their mom. She did what she needed to do to survive, just like they did. It was not Haven's fault—or his mom's, for that matter. It was just the nature of the game.

"Vance has connections, and I need those connections."

"What the hell for?"

"You just leave that to me, little bro. I have a plan. If we play this right, we might just make enough to keep us set for a good while."

Carl and Kelly found Vance Haven holed up in a rundown motel room three blocks from downtown. He and his whores were passed out and had no clue the world had gone to shit. At first, he was reluctant to give up any names. But after a little persuasion in the form of some heroin, Carl had the name he needed. Carl patted a big-breasted brunette on her naked ass as he left the room.

"Tell Vance that I may have some work for him if my little venture pays off," Carl said to her as he shut the door.

Vance was a pussy, but he sure could charm the ladies. He might prove useful in the future.

Terrance Wright was a huge man in both stature and status. His crew was not going to let Carl and Kelly get anywhere near their boss. Carl knew that, so he chatted up one of his low-level street runners named T-Man. He said he had a business deal that might profit the boss and wondered if he might be interested in hearing his proposal.

"Tell him I'll be at Bill Budget Inn if he's interested," Carl said.

Two hours later, a short African American man wearing a Cubs baseball hat and jersey knocked on the door to Carl's room.

"So, let me get this straight, you think you can keep the boss supplied in girls and find a way to move them up and down the routes?" T-Man asked.

"I know we can. How much would he be willing to pay per girl?" Carl asked.

The man hit a blunt, held it, and slowly exhaled. Carl nervously tapped his hands on his knees, trying hard not to scratch at the scabs on his face. The man pointed at Carl's face.

"You're a fucking junkie, how you gonna get girls? Look at that damn face, all scabbed up and shit."

"If I can bring him girls, what will he pay?"

"Well, before the world went to shit, it was a G, but if you can guarantee a steady supply, he might be willing to pay a little more. But only if they are quality. No scabbed-up junkies like you."

"What if I can find a way for him to move them too? How much would that bring me?" Carl asked, sweat breaking out on his face. He needed a fix in the worst way, but he needed to finish his business first. He'd celebrate big time if he could pull off this deal.

"How would you do that?"

"I wouldn't want to reveal my secrets before I have a deal. Just say I could. What do you think that'd be worth to your boss?"

"I don't know, couple large maybe. I'd have to run that by the boss and see."

"You do that for me, and I'll get you something nice to take to him as a show of good faith. Like a sampler. Will that work?" Carl asked, sucking on his lip.

He was doing everything he could not to scratch at his crawling skin. He wanted to look professional. The boss was known not to deal directly with junkies. Maybe if this deal became as lucrative as he thought, he'd kick the shit and become a stand-up business-man. Perhaps a rival to the boss. Hell, he had the smarts to be king around here if he wanted to. He just hadn't applied himself to it yet. Yet.

Carl had shot up and was resting when the door to his motel room crashed open. Kelly ran in, startling him.

"What the fuck, man? What's the hurry?"

"Jimmy," Kelly panted.

"Jimmy? What the hell about him?"

"He's on his way. He has his guys with him. I was over at Jenny's and overheard her brother talking about it. We have to go."

Kelly grabbed Carl's arm and pulled his brother to his feet.

Carl stumbled, nearly falling back onto the bed. Kelly put an arm around Carl's waist and helped him to the door. As they rounded the side of the motel, Kelly spotted Jimmy's Mustang coming down the street, weaving in and out of traffic.

"Shit, shit, shit. We have to hurry, Carl. Here comes Jimmy!"

Carl heard Kelly talking but couldn't make out his words.

Carl woke up with straw poking him in the face. He rolled over and vomited over the edge of the barn's loft. Kelly scooted over and handed him the bandana he carried in his pocket. Carl always thought it was odd that his brother carried one, but he was grateful for it at the moment.

"Where the hell are we?" Carl asked, laying back on his straw bed.

"Uncle Mark's barn."

"Why did you bring me here? You know that cocksucker hates me. He pulled a shotgun on me the last time I stopped by."

"That is why. I thought Jimmy wouldn't think to look for us here. He knows Mark wouldn't put you up."

"Hell no, he won't. He'd give me up."

Mark was his mother's brother, but they'd never been close. He resented her for making his parents raise two boys in their old age. Not that he ever lifted a finger to help them, but that was beside the point.

He was also a hypocrite. He talked shit about Carl and his mom's drug habits, but he was a sloppy, fucking, no-good drunk. He slapped his old lady around and lived off her family's money. No, he was no better than them, but he sure as shit thought he was. Carl would've liked to take him down a notch or two, but he didn't have time for that now. He had girls to find and money to make. Now, he'd need to find a new dealer too. Jimmy wasn't going to be selling him dope any time soon.

Carl sat up and tried to steady himself. His head was pounding, and his stomach cramped like he was giving birth. He rubbed his stubbled face, lifted his arm over his head, and sniffed his armpits. He shook his head and lowered it.

"I need a fucking bath. I can't even remember the last time I had a shower. Days, weeks, I can't remember. Anyway, we need to stop by and pay Pop a visit."

"What the hell for, Carl? You know he ain't gonna help you any more than Uncle Mark would."

"Well, I ain't gonna be the one asking."

Kelly looked at him. Carl flashed him a cheesy grin, his yellow and rotted teeth on full display.

Kelly shook his head.

"Oh no, I'm not going to go up there and ask him to help us. He don't care for me any more than he does you. He'll just slam the door in my face like he did the last time I paid him a visit unannounced."

"You aren't going up there to ask him for anything, stupid."

"I'm not?"

"No, you're going to tell him you were worried about him and came to see if he needed anything. Maybe offer to do some chore for him. Anything that will get us the key to the barn and inside without getting pumped full of lead."

"He ain't gonna fall for that. You know I am a terrible liar."

"We're gonna practice until you get it right, then you're sure as hell gonna go up there and get me that damn key," Carl snapped.

CHAPTER 11

San Diego, California
Event + 1 day

The sun was shining as usual in San Diego. Beth didn't think it should be.

The nation was in mourning.

She was in mourning. Her mother, Florence Elizabeth Evans Wilson, had died peacefully in her sleep.

Beth was relieved that her mother would not have to endure the agonizing pain of cancer without morphine. Beth was grateful that the nurse had left the small bottle of the strong pain medication. Her mother had one shot left. It had spared Beth having to watch her mother die an excruciating death. With the shelter-in-place order still in effect, the hospice nurse hadn't returned. The morphine pump had hung empty for more than twenty-four hours.

The coroner's office had finally come, and the funeral home had removed the body. Her mother would be cremated. Beth would be allowed to pick up her ashes when the emergency order was lifted.

Frank had retreated to his room upstairs. He hadn't slept in there since his wife had gone to the hospital the month before. Beth had tried to get him to come down and eat lunch, but he refused. She could relate to his need to withdraw. She had done the same when her husband had died.

Sitting in front of the television, Beth listened for any news from Illinois and Missouri. The information coming in was disturbing. The news showed a convoy of military vehicles heading into San Diego. Beth wondered why they wern't going to help keep the peace in the affected areas of the country.

The phone rang, and Beth nearly jumped out of her seat. It hadn't rung since the EMP had struck. Hurrying across the room, Beth yanked the phone from its charging cradle. She didn't even take time to check the caller ID. All she could think was that it could be her kids.

"Beth, Roger Miller here. I received the message you left last weekend. I'm sorry it took me so long to return your call. I was out of town."

Beth thought for a moment. Had she called Roger? Roger and Greg had been roommates when she met them. They had stayed close, even after Greg's death. She remembered wanting to let him know she and Maddie were in town. They always had dinner together when they came to visit her mother.

"Roger, hi. It's okay. Things have been crazy for everyone. I'm surprised to hear from you. Didn't your unit get deployed to deal with this mess?"

"No, I got out, remember? I have a job with a contractor as an urban reconnaissance and surveillance instructor."

"Oh. I remember you said you had applied. Congratulations. How do you like civilian life?"

"It was great until the shit hit the fan."

Beth fought back tears. The shit had, indeed, hit the fan, and all Greg's preps were of no use to her and her children now. He'd be so disappointed in her. When she booked her and Maddie's flight to California, it had never even crossed her mind that they would be leaving their get-home bags behind. It was her fault that her daughter was defenseless in an airport in Chicago.

"How's your mom? You said you and Maddie had come to care for her."

Beth could no longer contain the tears. She sobbed into the phone, unable to speak.

"Oh, Beth. I'm so sorry about your mom. If there is..."

"Maddie and Zach are out there alone. Maddie was on an airplane flying back to Ohio when the EMP hit. Zach is somewhere along an interstate in southern Illinois on a class field trip. They're helpless, Roger, and it's all my fault," Beth cried.

"I'm on my way. I'll be there in twenty minutes," Roger said.

"What about the travel ban?"

"Fuck it. They can shoot me. I'm on my way. Don't worry, Beth." Roger said, and the line went dead.

Roger dropped his pack and M-4 just inside the door. Beth stood at the end of the long hall. Roger turned to her and opened his arms wide. Beth ran to him and collapsed into his arms. She felt her knees buckle. He held her tight.

The grief of so many losses overcame her. It felt as if every cell in her body mourned. She felt the physical pain of grief. When Greg died, she'd thought she couldn't bear the pain. It was so intense that she wanted to leap from her body to avoid it. It was the kind of pain, both mental and physical, that she'd do just about anything to stop. And the only thing that'd make it stop was gone. Her husband was dead. Her mother was dead. Her children were alone in the apocalypse.

But she knew, like a severe injury or disability, she must choose to accept the pain and move forward with living or do nothing and let it engulf her and hold her in place until she was consumed by it. With Greg, she had eventually chosen to accept the pain and move on. She had children who needed her. She'd had no choice. There was nothing she could do to stop the pain from the loss of Greg and her mom, but she had children. Children who were out there somewhere, alone, and they needed her.

Taking hold of Beth's shoulders, Roger leaned back to get a look at her. He brushed unruly strands of blonde hair from her face, then clutched her tight to his chest. He had been like a brother to her, and she found momentary comfort in his presence. She allowed herself to be in that moment and to feel the relief of not being alone.

The two sat at the table talking about news reports and the disaster area. Beth had gone up to check on Frank several times, but he refused to answer the door. Jack whined and scratched on the door to her parents' bedroom. When Frank didn't open the door to let him out, Beth ascended the stairs and knocked on her stepfather's door.

"Frank, is it okay if I open the door and let Jack out? He probably needs to go outside."

She heard nothing.

Beth knocked again. This time a little louder.

"Frank?" she called as she reached for the doorknob.

Beth cracked open the door. Jack bolted out and down the stairs. Beth turned to follow him, but then turned back and pushed the door open a little wider, continuing to call her stepfather's name.

"Frank? I just wanted to check to see if you needed anything. Roger came over and…"

Standing in front of her parents' bed, Beth froze. Frank's lifeless body hung by a necktie from a hook over the closet door. Backing out of the room, Beth closed the door. He had made the choice not the live with his pain. She could understand his choice. He was with her mother now. She envied him.

It was the choice she'd likely have made if she hadn't had Maddie and Zach to think about. And then there was her husband, Jason. He was a good man. He had been good to her and the kids, but he knew nothing about surviving the apocalypse. He was even less prepared than Maddie and Zach for the new world. Her kids would have to come first. Poor Jason would need to fend for himself until she got her kids home safe.

Does that make me a bad person?

She imagined that she'd be doing a lot of things that'd make her question that before she reached her children. But didn't have time for self-evaluation. She knew what she had to do. She had two thousand miles to travel.

"Is everything okay up there?" Roger called from the bottom of the stairs.

Beth descended the stairs in silence. She felt guilty for being relieved that she could leave there and not feel she had abandoned a sick old man in the middle of the apocalypse.

Jack ran past Roger, bounding up the steps toward her. She bent down and picked him up.

"Now, what the hell am I going to do with you, huh?" she asked, stroking the fur out of his one good eye. Beth carried Jack past Roger and went into the dining room. Roger followed silently.

Beth sat with one-eyed-Jack in her lap as she and Roger planned how to go find her kids.

CHAPTER 12

Olive Street Christian Church
Marshall, Illinois
Event + 1 day

The reverend and his congregation were cordial but not as friendly as Zach had expected. The church's stove operated on propane, but the refrigerators did not, so breakfast that morning had consisted of oatmeal and juice. While most of his class had turned their noses up at the meal, Zach scarfed his down.

Fuel is fuel.

Zach's intention had been to head out at first light, but Mr. Dean had caught him before he reached the door.

"Not yet, Zach," Mr. Dean said, catching him by the arm. "The chief stopped by this morning. The Red Cross is going to be coming soon to pick us up and get us home."

"Are you sure they are taking us home and not to another shelter?"

"That is what the chief said."

Zach reluctantly agreed to stay with his class and wait for the buses.

His friends didn't appear concerned at all. Jacob and Connor were acting like it was a big party. Connor had his arm around a girl's shoulder, while Jacob was leaning in talking low to another girl. Zach thought it was funny because his friends hadn't given those two girls the time of day before the lights went out. Zach thought of that country line his grandpa had said, something about all the girls looking pretty at closing time, whatever that meant.

The reverend was in a whispered conversation with a man at the church's back door. The man's voice was raised enough that Zach could hear him but not enough to make out what he was saying. He could tell it was more than a friendly, shoot-the-shit conversation by the animated way the man threw his arms around and pointed inside the church.

"What is that about?" Jacob said, walking up beside Zach.

"I don't know. Maybe he wants to come stay here and the reverend said no."

"Maybe. It is a little crowded in here. Did you hear that they ran out of bottled water already? Sister Brown came through passing out styrofoam cups. She told everyone to write their names on them because that was all they had. We have to drink tap water from the sink," Jacob said, wrinkling his nose.

"At least you have water. The people on well water would love to have running water right now."

"How do we know that their water is drinkable? Who knows what all is in it. Could be lead like in Flint, Michigan. I never drink tap water."

Zach shook his head. Jacob could be so dramatic sometimes.

He'll be drinking worse than that before the power comes back on.

Zach wanted to tell him just how bad things were going to get, but Mr. Dean was right. If everyone knew, they would panic. It would be hard to control everyone after that.

85

A couple of church ladies set up card tables in a fellowship hall off the kitchen. They laid out board games and decks of cards to give people something to occupy their time. A cart of books was brought in, but they were all religious books so most of them remained on the cart.

Zach sat in the pew nearest the back door, looking at the group milling about the sanctuary. There were several mothers with small children and no one to help care for them. If the Red Cross didn't come, he wasn't sure how they could possibly make it home on their own with little kids in tow.

A man in a leather vest and pants watched a group of kids playing on the floor just outside the kitchen. A little girl ran after a toy that another kid had thrown. Before she reached the toy, the man scooped up the little girl and tossed her into the air. He sat back down in the chair, holding the child on his lap. The child wiggled and squirmed then began to cry. A young petite woman exited the kitchen door, ran over, and grabbed the girl from his arms. Hugging her tight to her chest, she shook her finger at the man.

"You fucking perv. You keep your filthy hands off my baby girl," she yelled.

She kicked the man in the shin. Turning, she stomped back to the kitchen, clutching the child in her arms. The other mothers flooded out of the kitchen, shooing their little ones away from the man.

He rose and walked over to a group of men by the front of the church. If the other men had seen the commotion, they didn't show it. It was possible that the man didn't know better than to pick up someone else's child, but Zach didn't think that was possible. The man was in his early thirties. He was young enough to know how it would be perceived.

The men with the pervert all wore leather vests displaying the same logo. From the man's confident demeanor, Zach got the impression he was the leader of their group. The man pointed to the game room, and the other men followed him.

The morning dragged on. It seemed to Zach like it had been days. He resisted the urge to check his watch every five minutes. When the church ladies called out that lunch was served, his male classmates were the first to line up. Zach was starving too, but at least he had finished all his breakfast.

Lunch consisted of peanut butter sandwiches and juice boxes. Zach felt like he was back in kindergarten as he stuck his straw into the tiny box.

The church must have dipped into the nursery's food stash, he thought.

He was grateful and all, but breakfast hadn't been filling, and one peanut butter sandwich was more of a snack to a teenage boy. His stomach rumbled loudly by two o'clock. He didn't want to risk being seen taking food from his pack, so he slung it over his shoulder and headed to the bathroom.

Zach passed Becket Hall's music teacher, Mrs. White. She glared at his pack as he passed. Zach gave her a broad smile.

"Where are you going, Mr. Langston?"

"I was just going to change clothes, Mrs. White," Zach lied.

"All right, you have five minutes. No playing around it there. You don't have cigarettes or anything in that pack, do you?"

"Gawd no. I just want to get into something more comfortable."

She nodded. Zach pushed open the bathroom door. Two men were huddled in the corner, puffing on a cigarette and blowing it out an open window. The church didn't allow smoking, of course. The men looked up, saw it was Zach, then went back to their conversation.

They don't consider me a threat. Good.

Zach entered a vacant stall and shut the door. He lowered the lid of the toilet and sat down. Placing his bag on his lap, he unzipped a top pocket. It contained energy bars and nuts. Knowing he needed to conserve food for his trip home, he removed only one energy bar and a small bag of nuts.

After slowly tearing open the wrapper, Zach peeled it back and took a bite. He ate the energy bar and a handful of nuts, then put the bag back into the pouch. Standing, he opened the stall door and slung his pack over his back. The two men turned and stared at him as he walked over to wash his hands. When he turned on the water, he remembered he had forgotten to flush. Looking at the men, he doubted they would think anything of him not flushing. But not wanting to rouse suspicion, he turned and walked back to the stall. Reaching in, he flipped the handle to flush the toilet. Returning to the sink, he washed his hands. He looked around for paper towels to dry them.

"Ain't none. They ran out early this morning. They said they don't got no more," the man with long, sandy brown hair and dirty jeans said.

"Oh, okay."

"Whatcha got in there?" the other man asked, pointing to Zach's pack.

The man stepped forward, dropped his cigarette on the floor and stamped it out with his foot. He too looked dirty and disheveled.

"Just books and clothes mostly. We were on a school field trip when this—whatever this is happened," Zach said, wiping his wet hands on his pants.

"Let's have a look," the first man said.

"Yeah, we need to make sure you don't have drugs or something in there," the second man said.

As the men rushed toward him, Zach hurried toward the door and opened it. He could see the men had gained on him. They were just behind him when he exited the bathroom. He turned to look over his shoulder and bumped into Mr. Dean.

"Whoa, slow down there, Zach. What's the hurry?"

"Mr. D, I don't think it is going to be safe here very much

longer. There are some sketchy-ass dudes staying here with us," Zach said, his voice cracking.

Mr. Dean took Zach by the arm and led him away from the restrooms. When they reached the back of the church, Mr. Dean turned to Zach, placing his hand on Zach's shoulder.

"Did someone do something to you in the restroom? You can tell me, you know."

"Oh no, Mr. D, nothing like that. I just have seen some sketchy behavior from some of the men here."

Mr. Dean motioned for Zach to take a seat in the last row of pews. Scooting in beside him, he said, "Tell me what you saw that concerned you."

Zach placed his pack on the pew beside Mr. Dean and turned in his seat to face his teacher.

"Well, for one, I watched that man over there in the leather vest pick up a little girl and put her in his lap. When she struggled, he held her tighter. Her mom had to come wrestle her out of his hands."

"That is concerning. I'll have a talk with Chief Baker about it. Maybe he can post one of his officers inside to deter that behavior," Mr. Dean said, standing to go.

"That is not all."

Mr. Dean lowered himself back to the seat.

"Go on."

Zach told Mr. Dean what had occurred in the restroom.

"We need to have a talk with Chief Baker. There might not be anything he can do, but he should be aware. He may want to at least have a talk with them."

Zach didn't think talking would deter those men. If the Red Cross didn't come for them soon, Zach feared that it would get ugly in the church by morning.

CHAPTER 13

Bellwood, Illinois
Event + 1 day

After witnessing the attack on the young woman, Maddie was determined to get away from the crowds on Mannheim Road. Exiting the parking lot, she chose to turn left toward a residential area. She doubted the men had gone into the neighborhood. All the action was centered on the stores and shops of the business district.

Although the residential area was quieter, people were still out on their front lawns talking to one another. Children played in the streets between stalled cars. Maddie and Emma walked along the sidewalk, scanning the road for any sign of the young woman's attackers. At the stop sign, Maddie had to choose to go right or left. Left led to a commercial district where she didn't want to be, so she picked right.

They walked three blocks before having to make another right/left choice. To prevent them from becoming hopelessly lost in the maze of streets, she decided this time it was best to check her map. Pulling it from the side pouch, she traced the route from the shops where they'd hidden behind the dumpsters to the residential street she had first turned on. Looking at the street sign above her, she retrieved a pen and circled it on the map. She traced a route that'd lead her back to Mannheim Road farther down in a less commercial area.

As she stowed the map back into her pack, a man dressed all in black passed them on the sidewalk. He didn't speak or look up. Maddie watched as he traveled down the street in front of them. Something about him gave Maddie the creeps. She hung back to see which direction he'd choose at the next intersection. About halfway down the block, two teenage boys stepped onto the sidewalk and walked toward the man in black. Stepping off the curb onto the street, the man continued to walk in the same direction. After stepping into the road, the boys kept advancing toward the man.

The man in black reached back and pulled a pistol from his waistband. Holding the gun down to his side, he kept walking. As he approached the boys, he put the gun back into his waistband but kept his hand on the grip. When the group met, one of the teens reached out and placed an arm around the man's neck. The man pushed the boy away with one hand, pulled his pistol with the other, then fired one-handed at each teen.

Pulling a gun of his own, the teen who had first approached the man began firing as the other boy fled in the opposite direction.

Maddie and Emma took cover behind a parked car. The teen with the gun ran right past them. Maddie peered out from behind the vehicle. The man in black dropped to his knees and fell face-first to the pavement. Rolling onto his back, he stared up at the sky. Looking up and down the street, Maddie could no longer see either boy. After the gunfight, the residential street was deserted. No one came out of their houses to see what had happened.

Straightening, Maddie pulled Emma to her feet. Standing a few feet away, Maddie could tell the man had been shot in the neck and abdomen. Wounds that, on a normal day, could likely be fatal. On a day without 911 and trauma surgery, his injuries were a definite death sentence.

Maddie stared down at the man. She felt paralyzed.

The man attempted to rise but could not. He tried to speak, but he only coughed blood. Maddie stepped closer. The man mouthed, "Help me."

"No one can help you," Maddie said.

A look of resignation came over the man's face. He looked skyward, appearing to make peace with his death.

Maddie looked to his right. A pistol lay by the tire of the nearest parked car. Stepping over the man, she bent down and picked up the Glock G42. She dropped the magazine into her hand. It was nearly empty. She laid it on the pavement and racked the slide, catching the ejected round as it flew into the air.

Maddie turned toward the man. He stared at the sky. She walked back over to him, knelt, and felt his pockets. In his left rear pants pocket, she found a full six-round magazine. Standing, Maddie slid the full magazine into the pistol, chambered a round, and ejected the magazine. She loaded the extra round into the magazine before slapping it back into the pistol. Gripping the gun, Maddie extended her arms into a firing position and felt its weight in her hand. It was light and would fit into a pocket, if she had a pocket.

Maddie smiled.

Dad would be so proud of me.

The gun didn't have a manual safety. She would have to be careful not to touch the trigger or let it catch on anything if she had to draw it in the heat of battle.

The man looked at her as she stood over him with his pistol in her hand. As she returned his gaze, they locked eyes. She knew he was dying, yet she felt no sympathy for the man. She looked up and down the street. Would she have to shoot anyone before she reached home? Could she do it if it came to that?

She wasn't sure.

Maddie carefully placed the pistol in the kangaroo pouch on her back. She reached back a few times to check how she'd quickly pull it if she needed to. It was likely to slide down into the pouch below her rain jacket and out of reach. In that case, she wouldn't be able to get to it without taking off her pack. None of the front or side pouches were big enough for the pistol. She'd need to find pants with a belt and deep pockets. Her tights and the tank top were a good choice for running, but not for carrying a loaded pistol.

The sun was starting to set behind the houses. It would be dark soon. She had hoped to be far from the city by dark. That was not going to happen now. She needed to find a place for her and Emma to hide until daylight. Looking around, all she saw was row after row of houses.

She took Emma's hand. They sprinted down the street, weaving between cars. Maddie slowed when they passed people in the road.

The two had traveled about ten city blocks before Maddie spotted the perfect place to stay the night. They ran down the block and through the next intersection. Just past the corner was a wrought-iron gate. Above the entrance was a sign that read, "Oakdale Cemetery."

Emma looked up, wide-eyed. As Maddie tried to walk forward, Emma pulled back, refusing to budge.

"Emma, this is the safest place in the city right now. No one will come into the cemetery and hurt us there."

Emma looked at the sign above the gate.

"It is just for the night, and I have a gun now," Maddie said. "Okay?"

Emma nodded. The two ran across the street, through the open gate, and down a paved walkway. At a stand of evergreen trees, Maddie ducked under low branches. After dropping to her knees, she held back the branches for Emma. The girls sat down and leaned against the largest of the trees. Emma laid sideways on the ground and closed her eyes

A rush of relief and then sadness engulfed Maddie. Pulling her knees to her chest, she sobbed quietly. She felt a sense of isolation and fear, unlike anything she had ever known in her life. Even more than the isolation she had felt in the last few years.

Although she came from a family of four, they lived splintered lives. Each tiptoed around, hiding their pain to spare one another. There were no more family camping trips, no game nights, no taco Tuesdays, and no more of Dad's swirly pancakes on Saturday mornings.

Zach had been the one to pick up their father's mantle. He had tried to be the man of the house. She and Zach had fought a great deal over his newly-assumed authority and him thinking he could tell her what to do. He was four years younger than her. If he grieved their dad, Maddie didn't see it.

But where she had felt fragile, broken, and abandoned, Zach appeared stoic, older, and wiser than his years.

Where is he now?

She tried to remember where he had said his class had stopped. He was at a McDonald's somewhere, she recalled. He was on his class field trip. Mr. Dean was pretty cool. He'd keep Zach safe. He'd know what to do. Mom was safe at Grand's. They'd probably be home when she got there. She comforted herself with those thoughts.

The lights might not even be out anywhere but here. They can't be off everywhere, or we are all screwed.

She awoke in the night. The exhaustion following the huge adrenaline dump must have put her right to sleep for a few hours. Stars showed through the branches overhead, and she was struck by the relative quietness of the night.

Missing were the noises of cars and sirens. Maddie heard nothing but an occasional crash and excited yells of nearby looters.

She could hear the occasional pop from gunfire in the distance. She sat still and quietly listened to the beginning of the end of society.

Emma lay curled in a fetal position at the base of her tree. Maddie removed a Mayday bar from her side pouch and ate it. She drank the last of the water in her soft flask and stuffed the flask into her pack. Her hydration bladder was empty. It weighed the most, but the mouth tube made it the easiest to drink from while running. She needed to find a water source quickly or she and Emma would be in trouble. With the cooler temperatures being weeks away, they would quickly dehydrate if they ran without water. The daytime temperature still reached eighty degrees in Chicago this time of year.

Unstrapping her pack and pulling it off, Maddie laid it on her lap. She carefully pulled out the pistol and put it on a rock beside her. From a side pocket, Maddie pulled the Ziploc bag containing her headlamp and water filter. With her water bladder, flask, and filter grasped in one hand and the headlamp in the other, Maddie crawled out from under the trees and stood. She looked around the cemetery.

The moon was half-obscured by clouds, but it provided some light. She stepped back onto the paved walkway. Not wanting to risk twisting an ankle stumbling around in the dark in a graveyard, she flipped on her headlamp, shielding its light in her closed fist.

Facing away from the street, Maddie flashed the light in front of her toward the trees she had just come from. From there, she shined the light right and left. Not seeing anything interesting, she turned to her left and shined the light in front of her and then to the right and left again. On her left, she spotted a small fountain in the cemetery's center.

"Yes!" she whispered.

Cupping the light in her palm and shining it on the ground, she made her way to the fountain. Using the Sawyer mini filter, Maddie filled her hydration bladder and all four soft flasks, giving her over two liters of water to start their run tomorrow. The mini-filter was slow, but it was lightweight—and a lifesaver.

Returning to where Emma lay under the trees, Maddie put the hydration bladder inside its sleeve, and the sleeve inside its pocket on the back of her pack. She pulled out her bivvy bag and placed it on the ground. Picking up the pistol from the rock, she shoved it in the kangaroo pouch beside her rain jacket. She removed the small folded emergency blanket from her pack and, after curling up next to Emma, unfolded and pulled at the super lightweight, loudly crinkling mass suspended over top of them, tucking it down and around their bodies. The soft bed of evergreen needles was comfortable, but she thought she'd think twice before calling attention to themselves with the loud, reflective emergency blanket unless she really needed it.

As she lay staring up at the stars that peeked between the branches above her, she thought of the camping trips she had been on with her mom, dad, and brother. Her dad had taken them to some exotic places, but never to a cemetery.

Most people, especially the girls she knew, would never spend the night in a graveyard, but Maddie was not superstitious. She had spent a lot of time in them since her dad had passed. Right after he had died, Maddie would sometimes sit at his grave for hours talking to him.

She had never wished harder that her dad was still alive. The first thing she'd say to him was that she was sorry for doubting him. The second would be to thank him for all he had done to prepare them for this world. She didn't know how she'd get home, but she hoped her dad would be proud of her for her effort.

CHAPTER 14

The Oakdale Cemetery
Westchester, Illinois
Event + 2 days

A light rain began falling through the boughs of the trees that Maddie and Emma lay under. At first, she pulled the sleeping bag up over her head, but then sat straight up, remembering where she was and what had happened the previous day. Maddie gently nudged Emma awake.

"Emma, it's daylight. We need to get moving."

Emma stirred, stretched, and sat up. Maddie pulled the weatherproof jacket out of her pack's kangaroo pouch. The pistol slid out and hit the ground. She had forgotten she had it. After wrapping the jacket around Emma, Maddie bent over and picked up the gun from the wet ground. She stared at the damp weapon in her hand. She had left her bandana with the girl back near the dumpster. Bending over, she wiped the gun on her shirt and carefully placed it inside the waistband of her running tights. There would be no way she could walk, let alone run, without the weapon falling out, but it would stay there long enough for her to pack up her bivvy and get her pack on.

Maddie rolled up the bivvy and stuffed it back in its pouch, then shoved it into the pack. Crawling out of the trees, she stood and pulled on the vest pack.

Emma crawled out and looked around the graveyard. After retrieving two Clif Bars and two bags of sports beans from the front pouch of her pack, Maddie threaded the mouth tube under her arm and secured it at her shoulder. Maddie leaned over to Emma and zipped the jacket to her neck. It hung below the girl's knees, and the sleeves dangled at her side. Maddie rolled the sleeves and pulled the drawstring on the hood. Emma wouldn't be able to move very fast with the jacket on.

Maddie removed the pistol from her waistband and placed it in the kangaroo pouch of her pack. She couldn't easily reach it there, but there was no way it would stay in her waistband.

Maddie bent over and did a few stretches before she and Emma walked off down the path and back onto the street. Hardly anyone was out on the roads now, whether because of the rain or because they had been trying to get home from wherever they'd been stranded. Either way, she was glad to be able to travel faster than yesterday.

Maddie had planned to spend some time that morning going over the map. She needed to familiarize herself with various alternate routes, but she didn't want to get the map wet. They needed to get off the street they were on. She was not sure if continuing to wind through residential areas would be wise—too many chances for running into dead-end streets and getting lost.

An hour later, the rain had let up and the sun was trying to come out. Maddie and Emma stopped at a small playground. Taking a seat on a bench near a slide, Maddie removed the pistol from her pack and laid it between her and Emma. After unzipping the jacket, Maddie pulled on the sleeves to help Emma take it off. She shook it to remove as much moisture as she could. Reaching over her shoulder, Maddie shoved the jacket back into the kangaroo pouch on her back. The great thing about the Salomon vest pack was she didn't have to remove it to reach most of the contents. She looked down at the gun on the bench. Reluctantly, she reached over her head and placed the pistol in the pack next to her jacket.

As they sat on the park bench, an old beat-up pickup truck backed out of a garage down the street and sped away. The door stood wide open. Maddie waited to confirm that the house was empty. When no one else exited, Maddie took Emma's hand. The two crept closer, making sure to stay behind the bushes that lined the street.

Maddie peeked over the top of the foliage. The contents of the house appeared to be strewn across the front lawn, making a path to the street.

The house had already been looted. She hoped the homeowners wern't home, for their sake as well as hers. Maddie looked inside the open garage door. On the back wall was a washer and dryer. Maddie and Emma ran to the corner of the house. Maddie leaned around and scanned the garage for the home's occupants. Not seeing anyone, she pointed to the garage. She and Emma rounded the corner and entered through the open garage door. Crouching beside a silver SUV, they made their way to the back wall. At the front bumper of the vehicle, Maddie stopped and listened. She peered around the car to make sure the space was empty.

Maddie motioned for Emma to stay put. She crept over and slowly pulled on the dryer's handle. The popping sound it made was loud in the stillness of the garage. Maddie looked over her shoulder toward the door that connected the garage to the house. When no one appeared, she opened the dryer to reveal what seemed to be a mixed load of men's clothes.

Score!

There were jeans and T-shirts. Maddie grabbed a pair of jeans and looked for the tag. They weren't ideal, but she could make them work. She'd make a belt from a length of paracord from her pack and cut the legs to her height. Next, she pulled out a large black T-shirt. She didn't need to look at the tag to know it was a large. It would do. Maddie had downsized many of her dad's T-shirts by cutting slits on the sides and braiding them. She slid the shirt over her head and pulled it down over her tank top. Reaching into the dryer, Maddie pulled out a handful of socks.

Yes!

She grabbed six white socks from the dryer. They were larger than her feet—and she knew of no way to make socks smaller—but they were clean and would have to do. Maddie reached back into the dryer. Using her thumb and index finger, she picked up a pair of men's boxer briefs. She wrinkled her nose.

"Ew. No freakin' way," she said under her breath.

"No freakin' way is right," Emma whispered, wrinkling her nose too as she looked up at Maddie.

She dropped them back into the dryer. Clean panties would be high on her list of must-haves for the next scavenging hunt. Crouching in front of the SUV, she slid off her running tights and pulled on the jeans. They nearly dropped to her knees. She scanned the shelves above the dryer. A basket sat on the top shelf. She pulled it down and dumped its contents on the floor. Under a pile of mismatched socks and items likely emptied from pants pockets lay a small pink belt. The socks were small. She held them up and looked to Emma.

"Will these fit your feet?" Maddie whispered.

Emma shrugged. Maddie stuffed them in her pack. She moved a few pieces of ripped-up T-shirt material and spotted what she had been searching for—a woman's belt. After threading it through the loops of the jeans, she cinched it tight. The fabric of the jeans bunched up in the back. There was nothing she could do about that. She removed the gun from her pack and carefully placed it into her right front pocket. She squatted down a couple of times to make sure it won't get in the way of running. She looked back at the small socks on the floor.

Maddie sprang up and opened the lid to the washer.

Tada! Miracle. Women and children's clothes.

Women's and a little girl's underwear and socks filled the washer. Maddie reached in and pulled out a mesh bag filled with bras and panties. Unzipping the bag, she pulled out a pair of Victoria's Secret, silky, red lace panties. They were her size too. Emma's eyes grew large as she glanced between the panties and Maddie.

Maddie smiled at her good fortune. Returning the panties to their mesh bag, Maddie zipped it shut and shoved it into her pack. She reached back into the washer and pulled out a girl's top. Maddie checked the size.

"Can you wear a medium?" she whispered.

Emma shrugged again. Maddie took a few. A large shirt was better than no shirt. Satisfied with her clothing haul, she turned her attention to a shelf of camping gear. She rifled through tents, a camp stove, sleeping bags, and fishing gear. She lifted a badminton racket to reveal what she had been looking for—a small hatchet. A hatchet was a great tool and could be used as a weapon.

Double score!

She opened a large tacklebox laying on the floor. It contained the usual lures, bobbins and hooks, and a filet knife. Maddie pulled the knife from its sheath and examined its edge, pleased with what she saw. Sheathing the blade, she placed it in the Molly webbing on the back of her pack. She now had two sharp weapons and a gun. Maddie looked to the door leading inside the house. She knew the house had been looted already. Weapons would have been the first thing they took—guns and drugs.

She stared at the door one last time.

Should I risk it?

"Stay here," she mouthed to Emma.

Emma looked like she wanted to protest, but she relaxed back into her position next to the tire of the SUV. Maddie scanned the garage as she walked toward the door. She reached out, turned the knob, and slowly cracked it open. It opened into what appeared to be a mudroom and pantry. Coats hung on hooks on one wall with a shoe-rack on the bottom. The shelves lining another wall contained large pots and pans. It appeared the looters before her hadn't bothered to go through this room.

On the same wall as the door was a shelf with gym bags and backpacks. Not little kid backpacks with cartoon characters either. Maddie opened the door wider and listened. Not hearing any movement inside the house, she pushed open the door. Before stepping inside, she looked over her shoulder and motioned for Emma to stay put. She left the door open in case she needed to make a quick escape. After grabbing a black pack from the shelf, Maddie set it on the bench under the coat hooks and unzipped it. Inside, she found the motherload.

Caffeine!

The pack had been someone's travel bag. Besides hotel soap and shampoo were bags of single serve coffee and teas. There was even sugar and creamer in the pack. Maddie grabbed the backpack and backed out the door. She wouldn't risk going in farther. It just was not worth it. They needed food, but she still had energy gels and sports beans.

Maddie emptied the contents of the backpack into her already overstuffed vest pack and motioned for Emma to follow as she crept around the side of the SUV and exited the garage. Looking around the side of the house, Maddie took Emma by the hand and ran to an abandoned car on the street. They ran across to the other side of the road. At the corner of the street, they turned left toward Mannheim Road again and the commercial district.

Back on Mannheim, the destruction from the looting and rioting the night before was everywhere. A few people still walked casually in and out of what few stores hadn't been burned. Maddie and Emma crossed the street to avoid a crowd in front of a boutique clothing store. A block from there, smoke rose from what had once been a police sub-station. Both girls stared expression-lessly as they walked by. It was a vivid reminder that the authorities were not coming to help them. Maddie had only seen one police officer since the shit hit the fan. Wherever the cops were, they were without a doubt unprepared for a disaster of this magnitude.

As they crossed over an interstate, Maddie saw a long convoy of military Humvees and trucks heading north into the city.

They've called in the National Guard, she thought.

They would need a lot more than what she saw to control what was going on in the city.

Maddie lead Emma behind a shopping center and the two took a seat on a short concrete wall. Maddie removed the map from her pack and studied it. With her finger, she traced a route heading south. They would need to go west soon to link up with Interstate 55. She selected two alternate routes, neither of which were really good options, as they wound back and forth through residential streets and would add hours to their trip. She was just about to the fold up the map and put it away when something caught her eye.

There was a gray line on the map indicating a bike or hiking trail. She traced it with her finger. The trail ran from east to west, and she needed to go west before heading south. She searched the map, hoping for a trail heading toward Missouri, but she found none. Uncertainty gripped her. Seeing the great distance she needed to travel was an eye-opener.

When she'd left the airport, she had only thought of getting out of Chicago and away from the craziness there. But now, realizing the miles she'd need to travel before she reached home and safety, she felt panic rise from her stomach into her chest. Her breaths came in quick bursts. Emma's big green eyes widened. Maddie closed her eyes and slowed her breathing, the way she did when she ran. When her breathing became slow and rhythmic, Maddie opened her eyes.

Patting Emma on the knee, she said, "It's okay, I just felt a little winded from all the running."

Her gaze returned to the map. Even though they had a little food and the means to purify water, they didn't have the gear to travel three hundred miles on foot, just the two of them, alone in the apocalypse. Her dad could have probably done it without a problem, but she was not her dad. Right then, she felt like a scared little girl. As scared as Emma likely was.

She needed to get moving and put distance between them and the city, but all she wanted to do was curl into a ball and hide until someone came to her rescue. Maddie studied the map again, hoping somehow there was a route that ran parallel to the interstate that didn't add extra miles to her trip. She looked at the Old Plank Road Trail once more and traced its path with her finger.

Maybe we can take it west for a ways, then find a route south.

She ran her finger from St. Louis up Interstate 55, searching for a better road to take that might intersect the trail at some point. It was then that a small town caught her attention. There, along another east-west trail, lay the city of Marseilles, Illinois. She could hear her mother's laughter when she had said that if she won the lottery, she'd take a trip to France. Uncle Ryan had offered to take her on a trip to this Marseilles instead.

"Um—no thanks. I want to go to France, not Illinois."

Maddie's dad had refused to take her mom to France, or anywhere that he couldn't carry a concealed weapon. Now Maddie understood, but at the time, she'd resented him for it. It meant long drives to the beach in Florida and even longer trips to California to visit Grand and Grandpa Frank.

She stared at the town of Marseilles on the map. Uncle Ryan lived near there. She had been there many times, but having never driven there herself, she never paid attention to how they got there.

She hadn't realized it was so close to Chicago. To her, it had felt like it was much farther north.

Depending on how far they still had to go before reaching Uncle Ryan's, she thought they could make it on the supplies they had. She thought of Uncle Ryan's famous firehouse chili. She was so hungry for real food that she'd even eat his awful tuna casserole...maybe. She may not be quite that hungry yet.

Uncle Ryan wasn't family by blood, but he was her dad's brother—a bond forged on the battlefields of Iraq and Afghanistan and, for them, a bond stronger than blood. He had been there for them after her dad passed away. He had made excuses to stop in, saying he needed to fix this or that. Maddie would come home from school, and Uncle Ryan would be sawing lumber in the back yard fixing their deck or cleaning leaves from the gutters. He was the family's rock. He'd held them together when her mom couldn't get out of bed to take them to school or to soccer practice. Uncle Ryan had been there for her in her darkest hour. She was sure he'd help her now too.

From the town of Marseilles, she traced another east-west trail leading to the city of Joliet. The Indiana and Michigan Canal Trail ran from the south of Marseilles to the southwest side of Joliet. When the Old Plank Trail ended on the east side of Joliet, they would need to walk the railroad tracks west, cross the Des Plaines River, and pick up the Indiana and Michigan Canal Trail south of Joliet. She calculated the distance.

The Old Plank Road Trail was twenty-two miles and then another thirty or so miles to Marseilles. It was a long way, but they could make it. Maybe not in one day, but they could get close. They could run some on the trail if Emma was up to it. The trail ran between housing subdivisions and through towns in places. That concerned her, but it was their best route.

Looking up from the map, Maddie spotted a small group of people sitting in the shade near the store. She watched them cautiously. As one of the men stood and began walking in their direction, Maddie reached over and grabbed Emma's hand. The girl looked up. When she saw the look of concern on Maddie's face, her eyes grew wide. She turned to see what Maddie was looking at. Emma jumped to her feet, but Maddie held her hand tight.

"Wait, Emma. We don't want to get into a foot race again." Maddie reached into her pocket and pulled out the gun. The man froze in place.

"Whoa, whoa there. I just wanted to see if we might be able to take a look at your map. We aren't from around here, and we have no idea where we are or how to get out of the city," the man yelled.

Maddie held the pistol down to her side and stood. She wrapped an arm around Emma and stepped in front of her. Emma squeezed Maddie's hand.

"If you stay on this road, it'll lead you south out of the city," Maddie said.

"Thank you," the man said.

He was short, maybe 5'6". He wore jeans, a polo shirt, and baseball cap. Maddie counted two women, two kids, and another male in the man's group. The woman and the two kids were bloody. Their clothes were torn. One of the women was tearing pieces of the other man's T-shirt and using them to cover a wound on one child's leg.

The man who spoke to her noticed her staring at the group.

"My wife and children were injured in a car crash. Our phones aren't working, and we haven't been able to contact anyone for help."

"There's been a terrorist attack or something. All the phones are down, I believe. I have a small first aid kit. Not anything like you probably need, but I have wrap bandages and antibiotic ointment," Maddie called.

"That'd help," the man said, taking a step forward.

Maddie raised the pistol and leveled it at the man. He shot his hands into the air and began backing away.

"I'm not a threat. I mean you no harm. I promise you."

"Just stay there. I'll toss the kit to you," Maddie said.

With her left hand, she reached back and grabbed the first aid kit from her pack.

Handing it to Emma, she said, "Open it and take out the Ace bandage and antibiotic ointment."

After taking the items from Emma, Maddie tossed them to the man one at a time. He thanked her and returned to his family. Knowing that she didn't have the physical energy to run should the men decide to chase her and Emma, Maddie sat back down on the concrete wall. Emma turned and looked at Maddie, her eyebrows raised.

"We need to eat something and get hydrated, Emma. We can't keep going if we don't."

Maddie set the pistol on her lap and pulled the sports beans and energy gels from her pack. Most of her energy bars were gone, but she had twenty gel packs and all her sports beans left. She added up the calories in her head and looked up at Emma. They would need to dig deep and push themselves hard. Maddie wasn't sure if Emma had that in her after all she had been through. But she had to.

Maddie looked at the man and his group. She wished they would leave first. She felt uneasy having to pass them. Emma took a seat next to Maddie. She sat so close that their legs touched, and Maddie could feel her trembling. Emma stared at her feet, quiet and expressionless. Maddie remembered that numb feeling all too well. She had felt the same after her dad died.

After eating and drinking, Maddie stood and took Emma's hand. She held the pistol down at her side and nudged Emma to move to their left, back toward the road. One of the women called after them. Maddie stopped.

"Thank you for the bandage. I really appreciate your generosity. My children are very thirsty. You wouldn't happen to have any water to spare?" the woman asked, standing to her feet.

Maddie's heart sank. She knew she should keep walking and ignore the woman's pleas for help. It was what her father had trained her to do, but her heart ached for the woman and her children. Being injured in this heat could be life threatening, and the water she carried could mean life or death to those kids. Could she live with herself if she walked away without helping them?

She thought for a moment. Making her decision, she reached into her pouch and pulled the two soft flasks out and laid them on the ground at her feet. She took Emma's hand, and the two girls stepped onto the sidewalk and crossed to the other side of the road. She fought the urge to look back as they crossed the intersection. Giving away two bottles of water would not have been much of a sacrifice just a few days before, but in the apocalypse, it could be life or death. But they had the means to purify water. Maddie had seen several ponds, rivers, and canals on the map. She felt good about her decision even though she knew it went against her training. She wasn't sure she'd have very many more opportunities to be so generous in the future.

It was a gesture that she intended not to tell Uncle Ryan about when she explained their journey. She could do without the lecture.

Maddie picked up the pace to a brisk walk, then a jog. They needed to get to Uncle Ryan. She hoped Emma was up to it. Maddie knew Emma couldn't run as fast or as long, but every step would put them closer. Uncle Ryan would help her get home. He'd also know how to get her mom and brother home. He'd know what to do about Emma. Uncle Ryan was like her dad. He was all go, no quit. She just needed to get to Marseilles and find him.

CHAPTER 15

Olive Street Christian Church
Marshall, Illinois
Event + 2 days

Things had gone from bad to worse in the cramped shelter at the Olive Street Christian Church. Tensions were high, and the stranded travelers were tired of the peanut butter sandwiches and water. It was impossible to sleep in the confined space with babies crying and all the snoring. Sometime in the night, the water had stopped flowing, so the bathrooms smelled disgusting by morning.

Zach washed his hands with hand sanitizer from his pack and tried not to touch anything, disease from surfaces touched by unwashed hands being his primary concern. Chief Baker was allowing small groups of the stranded travelers to walk down to the park to use the porta potty. Town residents had been brought down to the church to make sure that everyone went straight there and back. He was not allowing any of the stranded travelers to enter the town.

The chief had made it clear that they were not welcome. Mr.

Dean had told Zach that the chief was being pressured by concerned residents to make them move on. When Zach saw Mr. Dean huddled with Chief Baker that morning, he casually walked over, bent down, and pretended to be tying his shoelaces as he eavesdropped on their conversation.

"I'll hold them off as long as I can, but there's one group that I am concerned about. They have been lobbying the others and using scare tactics to gain support for pushing you folks out if the Red Cross doesn't come through today," Chief Baker said.

"Have you heard anything from the Red Cross or anyone from the government today?" Mr. Dean asked.

"The runner I sent yesterday said they were working their way down the interstates. They brought more buses to the region to help transport the interstate travelers, but they couldn't say how long it would be before they could make it here. He tried to get FEMA to give him some food and water to hold us over until they make it here, but they refused."

"That figures. If it is anything like their hurricane response time, we could die of thirst before they provide assistance."

"That aid would have gone a long way to ease the fears of the town about the safety of their own resources. Our townsfolk are a generous people, don't get me wrong, but they are scared. They are afraid that there won't be enough for their own families, so that is making them less willing to share with strangers."

"I can see how that'd be the case. I have a family. I would want to protect them too."

Chief Baker adjusted his belt and stared out the front door. The civilian crew he had brought with him to maintain order at the church stood eyeing the refugees with suspicion, their expressions unfriendly.

"Yeah, Lance Lucas and his bunch are stirring up fears with the talk of the power being out months to years and bands of roaming marauders coming to steal folks' food, which sure ain't helping the situation."

"There are always those fearmongers in every town, aren't there? They spread their doomsday prediction and recruit followers," Mr. Dean said, looking toward a group of men huddled in the front of the church.

"You got some of that going on here?" Chief Baker asked, nodding toward the men.

"I'm afraid so. I overheard them talking to some of the other men late last night. They were telling them that FEMA would come and put us all in concentration camps and encouraging each other not to go."

"What did they suggest people do, then? Surely they don't think they can stay here in the church indefinitely."

"I don't know what solutions they are advocating. When they saw me, they shut up and waited until I was out of hearing range before continuing their conversation."

"Well, I sure hope we don't have a situation when that Red Cross bus gets here. I can assure them, my town's folks won't tolerate no funny business. I'll do my best to keep the peace, but I only have so much manpower right now and no hope of backup from other police agencies."

"I just want to get my students and teachers on that bus and heading home before tensions boil over and things get ugly. I pray they get here before then."

"Me too," Chief Baker said, walking to the door. He turned and looked over his shoulder at the men gathered at the front.

"Me too," he repeated as he turned and descended the steps.

Zach looked up and locked eyes with Mr. Dean. Neither of them spoke. Zach stood and stepped toward him, but Mr. Dean turned and walked away.

Zach joined Jacob and Connor in the game room. They were playing a game of poker. Jacob put a stick of gum on the pile in the center of the table and turned over his cards.

"Don't say it, Jacob. Just don't say it again," Connor said, shaking his head.

Jacob leaned over and put his face near Connor.

"Read 'em and weep, sucka!'"

"You've got to be cheating, Morton. Do you have freakin' cards stuffed down your pants or something? The next time I see you scratch your junk, I'm going to knock you out of that chair."

Connor shook a fist in Jacob Morton's face, a broad smile plastered across his face.

Connor shuffled the cards and dealt each of them a hand. A small boy ran over and crawled under their table and across their feet before emerging and running from another boy. The kids' squealing was grating on Zach's nerves.

He pulled up a chair and joined the card game. He eyed the men huddled around the table next to theirs. They spoke in hushed voices, no doubt planning something not good, he thought.

"You in or out, Langston?" Connor called, pulling Zach's attention back to the game.

Zach looked at the cards in his hand, folded them, and placed them face down on the table.

"I'm out."

"You're a shitty poker player, Zach. You know that," Jacob said.

"Yeah, I don't have cards stuffed in my junk," Zach laughed.

Jacob stood and pulled on the waistband of his track pants like He'd pull them down. Connor stood and shoved him.

"Dude, don't embarrass yourself by showing all these ladies that you're really just a little boy."

Zach laughed so hard that he almost fell out of his folding chair. The men at the other table shot him the stink-eye, and Zach rolled his eyes at them. The largest of the men stood. Jacob and Connor had their backs to the man. The big man took a step toward Zach and bumped his shoulder hard into Connor's back. Although Connor was an inch taller, the man was broad and muscular. Zach thought Connor's mouth often made threats that his scrawny physique could not deliver. Jacob had saved him from a beatdown several times, but even Jacob was no match for the mass of muscle with his sights on Zach.

"Did you just roll your eyes at me, pussy?" the man growled.

Connor made the disastrous mistake of shoving the man from behind, barely moving the hulk but pissing him off for sure. The man turned his midsection and landed a punch in the center of Connor's chest. Stumbling backward, Connor tripped over Jacob's chair. Falling to the floor, he clutched his chest and gasped for air.

Jacob jumped the man from behind, placing his forearm around the man's massive neck. The behemoth slung Jacob to the ground in front of him and kicked him in the ribs with a large work-boot. Jacob grunted and curled into a ball on the floor just feet from Zach.

The man stepped over Jacob and was just about to grab Zach when Chief Baker and a sheriff's deputy stepped into the room.

"Freeze! Hands in the air. Step away from the kids. Do it now. Get your hands up. Do it now," the deputy barked, his taser pointed at the man.

The others at the man's table stood and backed away. The big guy raised his hands, but his gaze remained fixed on Zach.

"I said back away from the kid. Do it now, or I will taze you."

Something came from Zach's mouth that shocked even him.

"I'm sorry I disrespected you by rolling my eyes. My dad raised me better than that."

The man's gaze dropped to Zach's bag lying on the ground next to his feet. Zach looked down at his dad's Navy and Marine Corps Commendation Medal pinned to the strap of his pack. The man raised his head in an acknowledging nod and backed away while keeping his hands in the air.

Chief Baker rushed over and placed handcuffs on the man. He did not resist. They escorted him out of the building.

Connor milked his injury for all it was worth with the girls. Jacob sat with his arms folded across his chest, head down. Zach tried to tell him he had nothing to be ashamed of being beat by the man—the guy was at least a hundred pounds heavier than Jacob—but Zach realized he was only making it worse. They sat together on a pew in the sanctuary looking glum.

"Why did you apologize to that asshole, Zach?" Jacob asked, breaking the silence.

"I don't know. It surprised me too after I said it. I just— Well, I saw his tattoo, and I thought of my dad."

"What tattoo?"

"As he raised his massive forearm, I saw he had the Marine Corps' eagle, globe, and anchor insignia tattooed on his bicep. My dad had one similar."

"Yeah, but he was just about to wrap that big Marine Corps eagle, globe, and anchor around your scrawny neck and pop that ugly mug off your shoulders with it," Jacob laughed.

"I know. Sheesh, that was intense."

Suddenly, a loud explosion shook the church, startling Zach and Jacob. Jacob jumped to his feet, and Zach followed him as they rushed to look out the window. The two deputies who were guarding the church to keep the travelers in were now pointing shotguns at a group of town residents. They could hear raised voices but couldn't make out what the men were yelling.

The door flew open, and Chief Baker appeared.

"Everyone get downstairs to the basement. Now! Go, go, go," he yelled, waving his hands wildly.

Mothers grabbed their children, and an elderly couple struggled to get to the door through the crowd of people. Most of Zach's class just stood staring at the chief, stunned by the explosion.

Mr. Dean and the other teachers ran around grabbing students by the arms and pushing them toward the basement door. Instead of heading toward the basement, Zach, Jacob, and Connor ran over to the door. The deputies were fighting back a growing crowd of residents gathered outside the church.

"We want them gone, Chief. You said they'd be gone today,

and they are still here—and now someone done broke into my home and stole my rifle."

"Margrette's little girl said a man snuck into her room last night," a man waving a bat called out.

"He ain't gonna be breaking into any other little girls' rooms cause he's lying on my back porch with some new air holes in his belly," a short man in bib overalls yelled.

"You folks all just need to calm down. There are women and kids in that church. You people don't want to traumatize a bunch of already scared little ones, do you?" the chief said, waving his arms over his head.

The crowd all turned in unison as the big tour bus rounded the corner and pulled up in front of the church. The group stepped back and let the bus pull forward.

"All right, folks, as you can see, their bus is here and they'll be leaving soon, so why don't all you fine folks just go back to your houses and let us get them on their way?"

The sign on the bus read, "Red Cross." Zach had expected it to say, "FEMA." Zach wondered for a moment how they had working buses when no one else did. A second bus arrived as the first was pulling away from the church. They had boarded the families with small children and the elderly first. Zach and his class would fill an entire bus alone, so they would be the last ones picked up.

Zach had a funny feeling about getting on the bus and losing control of where he went. He debated with himself about heading out on his own now. It was the angry look on the faces of the residents that convinced him to stay with his class. People had already developed an "us vs. them" mentality.

Getting home by himself, having to walk through towns just like this one, would be dangerous. He could use backroads and go around cities, but without a weapon to defend himself, he'd still be at the mercy of anyone wanting to take his pack or hurt him for sport.

Zach boarded the last bus filled with his classmates and teachers and took a seat near the driver. As it pulled away from the church, Zach hoped it would head toward St. Louis and home.

CHAPTER 16

The Old Plank Road Trail
   Southwest of Chicago, Illinois
   Event +2 days

After scavenging a few outbuildings and the house near Mannheim
Street, Maddie and Emma had a jar of peanut butter and a package
of crackers to share between them. They jogged toward the trailhead of the Old Plank Road Trail, turned right, and headed west
toward Joliet.

Maddie had to keep reminding herself to match Emma's pace.
She explained to Emma the rhythmic breathing technique that her
running coach had taught her.

"Alternating footfalls and exhales helps prevent too much
repetitive force on your joints and helps control your breathing,"
Maddie explained.

Her dad had used a similar technique when he had run with her,
but his included his military cadence calls.

By the time they passed a row of houses that abutted the trail,
they were running at a good pace. Maddie heard children playing.

As they drew closer, a group of kids maybe eight or ten years old were playing in a yard. As she and Emma approached them, everything appeared quite normal. Maddie thought perhaps the lights were on here.

"Hey, kids, did your lights come back on yet?" Maddie asked, slowing her pace to a jog.

"Nope," said a sandy-haired boy holding a basketball in his hands.

Two little kids sat in a sandbox having a tug-of-war over a dump truck.

"I'm gonna tell Momma," the smaller of the two said.

"Momma ain't here, dumbass," said the older boy with the ball.

"Did your parents make it home?" Maddie asked.

"Nope. Jeremy's dad said that when the lights went out, all the cars stopped working. So, I guess Momma can't get home until the lights come back on."

Maddie nodded and waved as she picked up her pace. Two doors down, a gruff male voice called out behind them.

"Hey, pretty ladies. Where you girls running off to?"

Maddie patted the pocketknife in the pouch under her left arm, grabbed Emma's hand, and increased her pace. Maddie turned her head to check on Emma. She was pumping her arms and breathing through her mouth. She returned Maddie's concerned look.

Visions of the young girl being yanked off her feet by the men back by the dumpsters made her heartrate soar. She could feel she was reaching her upper limit. She was not properly hydrated and lacked the energy to push much harder. Emma was no doubt struggling even harder. Maddie started counting out loud to check her ability to speak and breathe.

"Count out loud with me, Emma."

Emma was having difficulty speaking. It was uncomfortable for Maddie, but she was still able to talk while she ran. They couldn't slow down yet. Not with creeper dude back there.

When they reached a point where Maddie felt they had put

enough distance between them and the man, she slowed her pace and returned to her rhythmic breathing. She was experiencing the after-effects of pushing too hard. She popped a couple of sports beans in her mouth and was relieved when she felt the caffeine kick in. She slowed and handed Emma a few sports beans and a flask of water from her pack.

The trail crossed over a city street, and Maddie instinctually slowed down and looked both ways to check for traffic.

At the city of Joliet, Maddie and Emma stepped onto the railroad tracks and crossed through town. It was much quieter than the streets in Chicago and its suburbs. Maddie spotted a roadblock of cop cars down one street and picked up the pace.

After crossing the Des Plaines River on the railroad bridge, Maddie and Emma continued walking south on the railbed. They took a water and bathroom break at the trailhead before picking up the Illinois-Michigan Canal Trail on the southwest side of town.

The trail ran alongside the Illinois-Michigan Canal. It looked like a creek to Maddie. Parts of the path were paved for a while until the path turned to crushed stone.

Trees, bushes, and tall grasses lined each side of the trail. The girls stopped in a heavily wooded area and took another bathroom break. Maddie checked their water supply and gave Emma her last flask. She handed her a packet of energy gel and several sports beans. Maddie popped several in her mouth, took the last sip from her water bladder, and got back on the trail. Maddie set a slower pace, knowing they were short on water. She was surprised that Emma never complained about the speed. Her feet must have been hurting.

As they ran, Maddie's breathing slowed and her mind drifted to school and her boyfriend, Lane. He had been there when she had crossed the finish line at the New Hampshire 100 on Labor Day. It had been three in the morning when she had finished the race, and she'd smelled wretched and must have looked her worst, but he grabbed her up in a big hug anyway. She liked him. There was a lot to like. Handsome, funny, and he supported her running. She wondered where he was and if the power was out on campus. Was there rioting and looting there?

She thought of her brother on the interstate with his class. Had they left the McDonald's before the lights went out?

Probably not... They had just gotten there.

She had just received Zach's text that he was in line for food before everything went dark.

Her mom was at her grandmother's. They were far enough away from any commercial districts back in their residential subdivision that if there was looting, it wouldn't be near them. She didn't know if her grandmother had passed away. How would they bury her if the power was out there? How was Mom going to get home? At least she and Zach were within a few days' walking distance from home. But her mom—she was too far away.

An explosion behind her made Maddie turn just enough to throw her off balance. She lunged forward, landing on her palms, gravel burrowing into her skin. Then her face bounced hard off the surface of the gravel path.

Sound was compressed, as if her head was inside a rubber ball, just before her vision faded to black.

CHAPTER 17

Grundy County, Illinois
Event + 2 days

Kelly knocked on the door of the old farmhouse. The rhythmic clack, clack, clack of Grandpa Goff's walker increased in volume as the old man crept closer to the door.

The clacking stopped, and the door slowly creaked open.

"What the hell do you want?" Grandpa Goff said, his wrinkled, weathered hand on the screen door handle to hold it closed.

Kelly looked down when his grandfather turned the lock.

He wasn't welcome here—but not for anything he'd done directly. It was a matter of guilt by association. He hadn't been the one who'd stolen his grandmother's pain pills when she was on hospice for cancer. That had been his brother.

"I just wanted to check on you. The electric is out in town and phones don't work. I wanted to make sure you were okay. See if you needed anything."

"Since when do you give a shit about me? What the hell do you want? I ain't got no drugs, so you might as well be on your way," Grandpa Goff said, stepping back and turning his walker around.

"Grandpa, I'm not Carl. I don't do drugs. I never took nothing from you. Ever. I really did just come by to check on you. See if you need anything. I know the well pump won't work without electric—and the microwave neither."

"Yeah, so what? What the hell you gonna do about it?" he asked, turning back toward the door.

"I could draw you up some water from the old spring and boil it for drinking. Grandma had me do that once when the storm blew that big oak tree over and the power went out. Then I could chop you up some firewood for the cook stove on the back porch. At least you could heat some soup if you wanted."

Kelly's grandmother had been raised during the Great Depression. When his grandfather built the farmhouse, she had insisted on a cooking porch, as she called it. It was a screened-in porch off the kitchen that held a large wood cook stove and a long, cast iron, double-drain board sink for her summer canning.

"You wanna do that for me…but what do you want in return?" his grandfather asked. The scowl on his face ripped at Kelly's heart.

Kelly fought the urge to fidget. It was his tell. Carl had helpfully tried to train him not to fidget by smacking him on the back of the head when it happened, but the method didn't produce much success. Kelly was mindfully concentrating to ensure he'd get it right this time. Besides, he did want to help Grandpa. They used to be close—before his grandmother died, anyway. Grandma and Grandpa Goff had raised Carl and Kelly until their mother was released from prison. Kelly had been eight and Carl had been fourteen then.

"I don't want nothing, I swear. I'll just go fetch you some wood and water and be on my way. You don't even have to speak to me if you don't want to," Kelly said, with a genuine hitch in his throat.

It had hurt him when he hadn't been welcomed in the house

after his grandmother passed. Everyone on his mom's side of the family treated him like he was the druggie. But Kelly was just trying to keep his little family together. He didn't find it as easy to throw away family members as they did. Yes, his mother and brother were junkies, but they were still family.

"You don't just throw away family," Grandma had said, when they'd talked about his mom and dad. She had understood, but the rest of her family didn't.

"Well, go on, then. Get the water and wood, then get the hell off my property."

"I'll need the key to the barn so I can get the wheeler out."

"Wait here while I fetch it," Grandpa Goff said, turning and shutting the door.

He had done it. At least Carl would be proud of him.

Carl rolled the ancient wooden door open as light flooded into the barn. Kelly doubted the four-wheeler would start on the first try. He doubted it had been started in years. The battery was likely dead, and the gas was old.

Carl walked over and flipped the machine's power switch on before swinging a leg over the seat. He turned the key, and, to Kelly's surprise, the engine not only turned over but also ran smoothly.

"Hook up the trailer," Carl called over the noise of the motor.

Kelly manually pulled the small trailer over, put the hitch down over the ball of the ATV, and cross-hooked the trailer chains to the receiver. Carl revved the engine and pulled out of the barn. Kelly pulled the door closed and hopped into the bed of the trailer.

Kelly hopped off at the back of the house. When Carl looked back and saw him standing next to the well, he circled back around.

"What the hell are you doing? We have to go."

"I said I'd get Grandpa wood and water. I'm gonna do that. It won't take twenty minutes, then I'll meet up with you where we planned."

Kelly never stood up to his brother. It usually didn't end well if he tried, and he hadn't expected this time to be any different, but this was something he had to do.

"All right, but hurry. We got shit to do," Carl said, accelerating toward the road.

~

Kelly stacked the split wood just inside the door of the back porch and put some thinner sticks into the firebox on the old cook stove. His grandma loved cooking on that stove. She said she preferred it to the new electric range she had in her modern kitchen, as she called it.

He thought, if the lights stayed off too long, maybe he'd come back and stay with Grandpa for a while. He needed more help getting water and wood, so perhaps Grandpa wouldn't turn him away next time. He doubted Grandpa would allow Carl to stay, but Carl had plans that didn't appear to include staying at Grandpa's anyway.

~

"Gramps, I lit the firebox and boiled a stockpot full of water. It is cooling on the counter in the kitchen next to the sink," Kelly said, poking his head into the sitting room at the front of the house. "You want I should warm you a bowl of soup or something?"

"Nah, I ain't hungry right yet. I'll get some later."

A box of crackers and a jar of peanut butter were set on a television tray next to the recliner his grandfather sat in.

"Okay then. I'll come back in a day or two and check on you— see if you need some more water and wood."

Kelly turned to go but stopped with his hand on the doorknob. He looked back at the room. It hadn't changed a bit since his child-hood. Their baby pictures still hung on the wall down the hall to his grandparents' bedroom. The fireplace mantle still held his grandmother's handmade doilies. The same quilt was draped over the back of the sofa that his grandmother had laid on the last time he saw her.

Tears welled in his eyes. He was happiest there. Happiness was hard to come by after his mother had taken him and Carl to stay in the endless string of gross motels, roach-infested apartments, and trailer homes where they lived with whatever boyfriend his mother was shacking up with at the time.

He had never missed his grandmother more. He looked back at his grandfather, who was staring at the blank television screen as if watching Jeopardy or something.

"I'll see you, Gramps," Kelly said, shutting the door behind him.

CHAPTER 18

I & M Canal Trail
Grundy County, Illinois
Event + 2 days

As Carl sped around the side of the old farmhouse, he looked back at his kid brother.

Twenty minutes, my ass. It'll take him that long just to chop the firewood.

Kelly was soft. He had rarely stood up to Carl. Carl could see that the world going to shit was getting to his brother. He'd give him time to be a do-gooder and take care of the old man. He knew his brother would need to harden up if he was going to make it through this mess—and Carl was determined to make that happen for the good of his new drug-and-whore enterprise. Kelly wasn't built for this new world, but Carl was made for it.

Carl barreled down the Illinois-Michigan Canal Trail as fast as the ATV would go. He wanted to stash the four-wheeler in the woods behind Taylor's Boat Shop before dark. He'd need to turn it off and push the machine for quite a long way to avoid anyone hearing the motor. He didn't want to fight anyone who might try to steal it from him.

As he slowed for a bend in the trail, he saw a black boy helping a tall girl onto a small trailer connected to an ATV. Carl turned off the key and coasted to a stop.

The girl appeared to be out cold as the boy lifted her onto the trailer. A younger red-haired girl jumped in with her.

If they had heard him drive up, they didn't acknowledge it. The tall girl in the trailer had nice long, lean legs and blonde hair. He waited, curious as to where the boy was taking her. After the boy started his four-wheeler, Carl started his ATV. Carl made sure he didn't follow too close. They exited the trail, crossed a road, and sped down a gravel drive. The boy pushed the machine to full throttle, throwing gravel as he accelerated down the driveway to an old yellow farmhouse.

An older woman raced from the front of the house. The smaller girl jumped from the back of the trailer. She helped the boy and the woman get the blonde girl inside. Carl knew he should leave—he had things to do and girls to snatch—but this situation piqued his interest, and he didn't know why.

Carl pulled his ATV into the bushes along the trail, well away from the farm. He didn't hide it well, but maybe if someone didn't look hard, they'd pass it by without seeing it. He walked along the tree line next to a fence running up to the side of the house. When he reached the back of the house, he crept over and peeked through a window. Seeing nothing, he moved to the back of the house and peered through another window. The woman was wiping what looked to be blood from the girl's hands and arms.

Carl couldn't see the girl's face, but her body was perfect. He briefly considered what had happened to cause her injuries, but he dismissed that line of thinking. He didn't have time for idle speculation. He needed to find his brother and get a girl over to Minooka as his first shipment to the boss. He didn't have time to waste.

Jimmy was looking for him, and that made moving around town more difficult.

After he made some quick cash selling a few girls to the boss, he planned on relocating somewhere out of Jimmy's reach. He had plans—big plans. He had the smarts to start his own operation. With the money he'd make from the boss, he could hire a crew and start his own business running drugs and girls. He'd been in enough outfits to know how to run a successful crew. He wouldn't tolerate the skimming he'd seen from Jimmy and the boss's crews. Hell, no. He'd shut that shit down hard. Maybe he'd grow large enough to take over the boss's territory. His mind raced. The possibilities were endless.

If the lights stayed out, that was.

Carl waited at the reconstructed Nettle Creek Aqueduct bridge for over an hour before Kelly arrived.

"What the hell took you so long?"

"I forgot they'd finished the bridge and reopened the trail. It has been closed so many years that I am just used to taking the road now."

"I almost just left your ass to walk back to town. Now, get on and let's get going. We got shit to do."

Carl and Kelly drove back to town and stashed the four-wheeler in the woods behind a boat repair shop. It was nearing dusk, and Carl was feeling sick from withdrawals. Needing somewhere to get high and crash for a while, Carl decided to wait until after dark to venture back into town and continue his search for girls.

The pair walked behind the garage to a boarded-up trailer home. Carl used a pry bar he had brought from his grandfather's barn to dislodge the 2x4s nailed across the front door. Inside, Carl flopped on the sofa while Kelly pulled a twin mattress from a bed into the living room. Carl lay back onto the couch while Kelly curled up on the mattress, and the two men slept.

"What the fuck, man. It is daylight already. You fell asleep, didn't you? I told you to wake me up in two hours so we could hit the streets. Mother fuck! Jimmy could have shown up here last night wanting his money," Carl ranted as he pulled on the doorknob.

Kelly jumped to his feet and followed his brother out and down the street toward the commercial district.

Carl selected the stretch that housed the real estate company, a bail bondsman, and a liquor store. On the opposite side of the street there was a bar, a hair salon, and a dry cleaner. It didn't appear that the shops on that side had been touched, but the liquor store was trashed. Nothing much was happening on that end of town, so the pair headed toward the Big Saver grocery store.

The pair stalked their prey like lions on the savanna. Person after person entered and exited the store. Finally, Carl saw what they were waiting for and motioned for Kelly to follow him.

This girl was a little older than the girl at the convenience store yesterday, and not quite as pretty, but she would do. The girl turned down the alley between the floral and pastry shops, and that was when Carl made his move. He took off at a sprint and disappeared down the next alley with Kelly struggling to keep up. Carl stopped at the end with his back against the wall. Kelly followed Carl's lead and took his place next to his brother, and they waited to make their move.

As soon as the girl's foot appeared, Carl lurched from his position and grabbed her from behind as she took another step. He slipped his hand over her mouth as she dropped the food she'd been carrying and reached for his hand.

"Grab her legs, Kelly," Carl yelled to his brother.

The two men carried the struggling girl down the alley and

through a side yard. She was getting quite heavy, and her flailing made Kelly lose his grip a few times as they made their way to where they had stashed the ATV. After tossing the struggling girl onto the trailer, Carl held her down, and Kelly mounted the ATV and fired-up its engine. When Kelly twisted the throttle, Carl and the girl quickly became more preoccupied with keeping themselves inside the bouncing, clattering trailer than maintaining their roles as captor and captive. They raced toward Jefferson Street, hitting every pothole as the four-wheeler threw gravel and mud at its passengers.

Boss's guy was pleased with the muddy gift. He examined her like she was a luxury car. The girl cried and swatted away his hand as he groped her.

"She'll do. Boss said he'd pay you two hundred dollars per trip for you to haul them up to Chicago. There will be trips south to Missouri, but he has to get in contact with his buyer down there to see if he's still in business now that the trucks won't run," T-Man said.

Carl counted out the money as they walked back to the ATV.

"How are we supposed to get those girls to Chicago and St. Louis?" Kelly asked. "The cars don't work, and the roads are a mess even if they did."

"Grandpa Goff's boat stupid. We can travel the canals and river all the way, back and forth. His old trolling motor should work since the ATV does. We just have to throw the boat on the trailer and head off to the canal."

"What about the locks?"

"The boat is light enough we can portage around them as we do when the water gets low on the river."

With his gift delivered, Carl set out to find more merchandise to pay his debt to Jimmy. It didn't take long. It appeared that the whole town was out shopping since everything was free. When Carl spotted twin girls together, he pumped his fist in the air.

"BOGO sale," Carl said, nudging Kelly with his elbow and flashing a yellow, toothy grin.

"What the hell is BOGO?"

"Buy one, get one free, stupid."

The twins proved a bit more difficult for the brothers to handle. They put up quite the fight until Carl pressed his pocketknife against the neck of one and told the other he'd kill her sister if she didn't stop. The other one gave up all struggle and did as she was told. He had been afraid of nicking the merchandise, but he found he didn't need to press that hard to get his point across.

There was just something about a shiny, sharp object that struck fear into the hearts of most people—at least in his experience. He thought this likely scared most people more than even a gun. Not that he'd had much experience with pulling guns on people. No. He preferred a knife over a gun. Carl liked the feel of a knife in his hand. He felt it was much more personal to be up close to his prey. He had more control that way, and it typically worked like a charm.

After delivering the twins, collecting his cash, and sending Kelly to pay Jimmy, Carl was in the mood to celebrate. Only, he didn't have anything to celebrate with. He stuck around after Jimmy and his crew went inside to borrow some from Jimmy's stash. He'd likely have a few hours of being back in Jimmy's good graces before he had to run from him again. Jimmy may not even connect him to the theft…again. If he was lucky, anyway. Luck might just be coming his way, for a change.

As he lay on the sofa in the trailer home behind the garage coming down from the rush, Carl thought about the girl in the yellow farmhouse. He knew she'd bring good money—and it might get a little hot for him when Jimmy discovered all the drugs in his tacklebox missing again. He could grab the girl in the farmhouse, sell her to the boss, and then move over to Shorewood, because the way things were unfolding, Jimmy wouldn't know where Carl went. If things didn't improve with the electric and all, he could set up his own little kingdom in Shorewood or somewhere else.

Hell, yeah—that sounded like a plan!

"Kelly, get up. We're going back to that farmhouse."

"But it isn't even daylight yet."

"We have to get guns first. We can hit them first light."

"Where are we gonna get guns from at this time of night?"

"Uncle Mark's, of course."

"You can't just go up in there and ask him to give you guns. He'll shoot your ass, and you know it." Kelly said, a narrow frown forming.

"I ain't walking up in nowhere. I am going to start a diversion, and you're going to do it."

"Oh, hell no, brother. You want to get me killed. Ain't no freakin way I am walking in Mark's house and stealing from the man. You know well as I do, he will hunt us down and shoot us in the street. No, with no law 'round, ain't nothing to stop him."

"That is why I'm gonna create a diversion. He won't know who stole his guns."

At Mark's barn, Carl pried-off the entire swivel hasp and padlock securing the door to the jam. The dirt muffled the clanging metal contraption after it and its rusty screws were freed from the weathered barn wood.

The boys found a gas can, some rags, and some old bottles, and they got to work. They filled the bottles with gas, and Carl sent Kelly out to get in place for his mission. Carl ripped strips from the rags, shoved them into the mouth of each bottle, and pulled his lighter from his pocket.

"Okay, Kelly, you better be in place. Don't let me down, bro," Carl said out loud to himself.

One after the other, Carl lit each rag, tossed the burning cocktail onto a pile of hay, and ran out of the barn. He dove into the bushes that lined the driveway just as the screen door slammed into the side of the house, announcing the arrival of his aunt and uncle. They burst from the doorway and shot onto the lawn in harried excitement.

Their screaming aunt was running in circles, arms flailing, and Mark was stopped in the middle of the yard with his hands on his head, yelling for her to get the garden hose.

Carl saw Kelly scamper from the bushes and dart across the driveway. He sat, regaled by the pandemonium, and nervously picked at scabs on his arms while he waited for his brother to return.

In less than five minutes, Kelly hustled back across the driveway and made his way behind the row of bushes, gasping for air.

A broad smile crossed Carl's face.

My plan worked perfectly!

CHAPTER 19

Grundy County, Illinois
Event + 2 days

Maddie came to with a pounding headache and opened her eyes. She was in bed, but not her bed. She turned her head and surveyed the room. Moving her head made her feel dizzy. The walls of the dimly lit room were a pale yellow and had photographs of flowers hanging on them. A mirror hung on the back of the door. The light coming from the open window revealed framed photos standing on a six-drawer dresser. She looked down at her body. She was covered with a yellow-and-blue quilt. She tried to sit up, but her head swam. She felt nauseous. She lay her head back onto the fluffy pillow and took some deep breaths.

The door opened, and the face of a middle-aged woman appeared in the crack, followed by Emma crawling under the woman's arm and rushing to Maddie's side.

"You're awake," the woman said, opening the door wider. "How you feeling? You feel up to something to eat or drink?"

Maddie tried again to sit up, moving a little slower this time.

Emma helped her pull back the covers. Maddie threw her leg over the side of the bed. Emma pulled on Maddie's arm, but she was still unable to get to her feet. The woman rushed in and reached for Maddie's other arm to assist her into an upholstered chair in the corner of the room. The room spun, and Maddie felt nauseous again. Bending over in the chair, she put her head between her knees.

"You feeling sick?" the woman asked as she placed a small metal trash can in front of Maddie.

"Where am I?" Maddie croaked.

"Grundy County—just outside of Inola. My boy found you unconscious on the trail. You must have fallen and hit your head. Your hands and face are pretty scuffed up. I cleaned them best I could."

"Thank you."

"You should try to drink some water. You might have passed out from dehydration. It is pretty warm out today. I'm Darlene, by the way."

"I'm Maddie."

Darlene picked up a glass of water from the bedside table and held it out. Taking the glass, Maddie drank a sip and placed it on the table beside the chair.

"Do you know what is going on out there?" Darlene asked.

"Yes. Emma and I came from the airport. It is bad out there."

"With the electric out, we haven't heard any news. Even our battery-operated radios don't work."

"We were at O'Hare when the lights went out. When planes started colliding above the airport and crashing onto the runway, I knew I needed to get as far from there as possible."

Maddie sat up, picked up the glass of water from a side table, and took a sip. She looked at the woman. She was older than Maddie's mom, in her late forties or early fifties. Her brown hair was graying, and crow's feet framed her kind eyes.

"Do you know what happened? Is it terrorists?"

"I don't know. I didn't see anything like bombing or anything. I saw a lot of looting and people doing really awful things. We saw the National Guard heading into the city."

Maddie ran a hand through her hair. It was like a rat's nest caked with dried blood. She touched her face and winced. She didn't even want to look at how bad it was. She had seen lots of runners do faceplants. She knew how bad it could be. It hurt like hell, but she didn't think she had broken any bones. She looked at her palms. They were bandaged with gauze and tape.

"I cleaned them up best I could. There might still be some sand and tiny gravel in them. A couple of the gashes were pretty deep. Your elbows were pretty bad too. Looks like you tried to catch yourself with your hands."

"Thank you for bandaging them."

Maddie couldn't help herself. She pulled up a corner of the bandage on her left hand to take a peek. It was as bad as she expected. They would swell. She'd had this happen before.

"You feel up to coming down for some dinner?" Darlene asked.

"I think so."

Darlene took hold of Maddie's forearm, trying not to touch her hands or elbows. Emma took the other. As Maddie stood, Darlene steadied her until she caught her balance.

"Now take it easy. A concussion is nothing to mess with. My boy, Ray Junior, he has had a couple of concussions, and we learned that you have to take it slow or you'll pay the price."

Darlene warmed homemade soup on a Coleman stove in the back yard and poured some into a mug for Maddie. Across the long farm table from her was a boy of maybe twelve or thirteen. He looked nothing like Darlene. His skin and hair were dark.

"This here is my boy, Ray Junior. He's the one who found you on the trail."

"I'm sorry I scared you," the boy said, his voice timid and low.

Maddie remembered hearing a gunshot before she fell. She looked up at the boy as he hung his head, looking into his bowl.

"What were you shooting at?"

"A rabbit," he said, lifting his head as broad grin crept across his face.

"Did you get him?"

"Yep. That is what is in the soup," he said with pride.

Emma set her spoon down with a thud. Her face was drawn up and her eyebrows furrowed.

We'll all be eating lots of things we found gross before things return to normal, Maddie thought.

"It is tasty," she said, smacking her lips.

She thought it tasted just like chicken. She had never had wild rabbit before. She had heard that some wild game like rabbits and squirrels tasted like chicken, but until now, she had thought it was a joke.

Darlene placed her mug down on the table and slid in beside Ray Junior.

"I guess if the power don't come back on soon, we're going to have to cook up the meat from the freezer before it all goes bad. That sure is going to suck to have to throw away all that beef, chicken, and pork."

"And my deer," said Ray Junior.

Maddie wiped broth from her chin with a paper napkin and placed it in her lap.

"You should start canning it now."

"Can it? I got a whole freezer full from when we butchered a steer and half my chickens, not to mention the summer fruit and vegetable from the garden. Most of that was canned, but the berries, peaches, along with peas and squash, well, I froze those. There's probably half a hog left from the butchering last spring."

Darlene lifted her mug to her lips, took a sip, and held the cup to her mouth as she stared off into the kitchen, lost in thought.

Maddie looked at Ray Junior. He was a thin, scrawny boy, but he could hunt and probably fish. They would likely do okay even without a freezer full of food. But if the power stayed off, they would need all they could get for the harsh Illinois winter.

"You could dehydrate the vegetables and make jerky of the meat. At least they won't go to waste."

"You think the power will be out that long?" Darlene asked, her voice pitchy.

"If it is out because of what my dad called an EMP or CME—electromagnetic pulse or coronal mass ejection—then, yes, it could be out for months."

"What is an electronic magnet pulse?" asked Ray Junior.

"An electromagnetic pulse. It's caused by a nuke being set off in the atmosphere. It sends energy waves or something crashing to earth, basically frying anything electrical or electronic like radios and things."

It occurred to Maddie that she hadn't felt naked without her phone as she'd have normally. Like most everyone else, she was never without her phone, usually checking her social media feeds every hour at a minimum. She even did her homework on her phone many times.

Darlene picked up her mug from the table and stood.

"Well, I guess I better get busy figuring out how to dehydrate three hundred pounds of meat and vegetables."

They spent the day preserving the food from the freezer. Maddie's headache was just about gone, but the cuts to her hands and elbow still hurt. Darlene and Ray Junior seemed like good people. Maddie and Emma liked them. The four of them had worked past dark constructing a smoker out of scrap lumber that Darlene's husband kept behind the barn. Scrounging in the family dump, Ray Junior found grates from long-abandoned barbeque grills. Maddie showed them how to build a firebox to attach to the smoker and how to hang the meat on the racks for drying. Darlene cut a roast from the refrigerator into strips and soaked them in brine, readying them for their turn in the smoker. The meat from the freezer would last a few days before the freezer temperatures dropped enough to start thawing its contents—as long as they kept the door closed. They removed the frozen fruits and vegetables to defrost first, because they would be first on the list to dehydrate.

While Ray Junior chopped wood for the smoker, Maddie and Emma cut up the vegetables as they thawed. Maddie taught them how to take the screens from their windows to use as drying racks. Darlene and Ray Junior had stared at her like she had two heads when she suggested they lay the vegetables and fruits out on the screens and place them in the junk cars on the property. There sure were enough of them to get the job done. Maddie thought Darlene's husband must be an aspiring salvage yard manager with the number of broken-down cars out beside the old wooden barn.

"Where did you learn this stuff?" Ray Junior asked, wiping sawdust from his pants. Maddie stopped chopping and placed the knife on the cutting board. A pang of grief gripped her heart, and she couldn't speak for fear of bursting into tears. The grief that she had so successfully suppressed in the three years since her father's death had been an ever-present companion since the lights went out.

"My dad."

"Your dad must be pretty smart. Where's he at?"

The words caught in her throat, and Maddie could not speak them. Those two damn words had replayed in her head over and over—the two worst words in the world. Maddie swallowed hard, fighting back the tears that were forcing themselves forward.

"He's gone."

She said it. She said it out loud. It felt as raw and painful to her as the day she had heard her mother say them. "He's gone. Your daddy is gone."

Tears streamed down Maddie's face, and she wiped them with the back of her hand. She looked to the sky, willing them to stop.

Blurring her vision, they flowed against her will. Emma flung her arms around Maddie's waist. The two of them wept. Maddie patted Emma on the back, feeling the girl shuddering in her arms. She stroked Emma's hair and rocked her gently. Maddie stared down at a colorful braided rag rug on the floor by the old porcelain sink. The wood floor bore the scars of many years of use. A path had been worn by decades of feet traveling from the back door to the living room. It reminded her of Uncle Ryan's house.

Releasing Emma, Maddie turned and walked into a tiny bathroom off the kitchen. Shutting the door behind her, she slumped down to the floor and wept like she had the day her dad had left her.

Maddie washed her face in a bowl of water Ray Junior had drawn from the well. The water was cool and felt refreshing on her sweaty, tear-stained skin. She blew her nose with toilet paper. It wouldn't be long before tissue, paper towels, and toilet paper were a luxury that few, if anyone, would enjoy. Maddie stared at herself in the mirror. Her left cheek was bruised and swollen. Her top lip was scraped, and her chin had abrasions. But it was the huge bags under her eyes that caught her attention. A good night's sleep was another luxury that few would enjoy from now on.

When she opened the door to the bathroom, Ray Junior stood in front of her.

"I'm sorry I made you cry."

"Oh, buddy, you didn't make me cry. I just miss my dad."

"I miss my dad too. I hope he'll make it home soon."

"I am sure he's doing everything he can to get back here to you and your mom. From what I can see around here, your dad is a pretty resourceful guy."

Maddie patted Ray Junior on the shoulder and returned to chopping vegetables. Emma sat on the rug, stroking the head of a big white dog in her lap. Emma smiled and kissed the dog as he rolled over to have his tummy rubbed. Maddie looked out the kitchen window into the back yard.

Ray Junior opened the back door. The dog stood.

"You can stay, Coop," Ray Junior said to the dog.

The dog returned to his previous position in Emma's lap.

"Mom don't usually let Cooper be in the house. He's supposed to stay with the goats. It's his job to watch over them, but he wanders off a lot. Daddy says he's patrolling his territory for threats, but Momma thinks he's off looking for a meal from the neighbor. Old Mr. Jenkins feeds him jerky."

"I'd wander off for jerky too," Maddie said.

"Well, after y'all get done with the veggies and start cutting up the meat, you won't have to wander too far too soon."

"I can't wait!" Maddie said.

"I best get to chopping some more wood. Looks like we're gonna need a ton of it to smoke everything in the freezer," Ray Junior said as he closed the screen door.

Returning to the task of cutting vegetables, Maddie watched Emma playing with the dog. She thought of her mom and brother as she chopped. All those weekend drills hadn't been for nothing. She and Zach had rolled their eyes when their dad would declare, "One more time." He'd have them repeat tasks over and over to create muscle memory. At the time, all she had wanted to do was forget. She didn't want her muscles to remember the ache and pain of carrying that heavy pack up and down the hills or the cover-and-concealment drills.

Maddie's mom, Beth, hadn't been eager to create muscle memory, either. She went along because she knew her husband was passionate about it. But Maddie had heard her telling a friend that she thought it comforted him and gave him something to focus on. Beth believed it helped with his PTSD. She had said that all the ugly he had seen in the war made him want to protect his family, and she wouldn't fault him for that.

"Besides," she had said, "at least he's spending time with his kids. Lord knows he was away from them most of their lives. They deserve some of his attention now."

Mom will make it home.

All that time sweating and freezing in the woods and marching down backroads hadn't been for nothing. Dad had known what he was doing. He had prepared them for this world even though they had stopped drilling after he passed. To her surprise, she remembered the things he'd taught them. She remembered, and so would Zach and Mom.

Maddie was jolted out of her thoughts by the screen door closing hard into the jam with a bang.

"I'm ready for the next batch if you have enough cut," Darlene said, placing a large empty bowl on the kitchen island.

Darlene brushed a loose strand of her salt-and-pepper hair from her face. She wiped perspiration from her brow with her apron.

"I just can't thank you enough for helping us out like this. You've saved us a fortune in groceries. There's no way we'd make it this winter, power or no, without the food from that freezer."

"It's my pleasure. You took us in and bandaged me up. If Ray Junior hadn't rescued me, there's no telling who might have come along and done who knows what to me laying there unconscious like that."

Maddie placed the knife on the cutting board and looked at Darlene. The woman's wrinkled mouth formed a smile. Her eyes beamed with pride.

"He's such a good boy. I couldn't ask for a better son. He ain't nothing like those other teenagers at his school. He's kind and cares about people. That boy never complains about doing chores around the farm—even the stinky, messy ones. With Ray on the road most of the time, Ray Junior steps up and takes care of what needs doing. We're darn proud of him."

"He's a very sweet boy. My brother, Zach, sort of stepped up when my dad died. He was only eleven, but he took on a lot of Dad's chores. He even tried to boss me around. I think he resented when my Uncle Ryan came around to help out, because he felt it was his job and Ryan was stepping on his toes."

"Yeah, I think boys somehow believe they have to grow up and take care of things when the dads aren't around," Darlene said, scraping squash into a bowl.

Maddie thought about that a moment. She hadn't seen it before, but Zach had grown up faster than other boys his age. When his friends had been interested in playing baseball and video games, Zach had been fixing broken faucets and cleaning the gutters, even after their mother remarried. Jason was worthless when it came to fixing stuff. They both had grown up too fast. It wasn't supposed to be that way. But they'd need to grow up even more quickly now.

CHAPTER 20

Red Cross Disaster Shelter
  Decatur Airport
  Decatur, Illinois
  Event + 2 days

As Zach had feared, the bus hadn't headed west on Interstate 70. Instead, it traveled north. Zach was sure that he had made the wrong decision when the bus stopped at a gate guarded by armed soldiers. His dad hadn't spoken about camps or what would happen to stranded travelers in an end-of-the-world-as-we-know-it scenario, but Zach had read about it in his research. A lot of the YouTubers had talked about FEMA's plans for internment camps, much like the ones that held the Japanese during World War II.

Zach had read about camps being built in every state. He had even tried to get his mom to take him to Grandview, Missouri, to see for himself if the rumor of a FEMA camp there was true. The camp for Illinois was supposed to be near Marseilles, where his dad's best friend, Ryan, lived.

Ryan had refused to answer any of Zach's questions about its existence when he had last spoken to him about it. Zach didn't understand why Ryan was shutting him down like that. Ryan and his dad thought alike, and he should have known why Zach needed to confirm its existence. He lived right there next to one. Why, if it was just a conspiracy theory, had Ryan not jumped to debunk it?

The bus door opened, and a guard stepped in. The bus driver handed him a piece of paper. The guard handed the note back, stepped off the bus, waved them through as the tall chain-link gates opened, and the bus rolled forward.

They stopped at another gate to another fenced-in area where several tall, white tents were all connected by what looked like tunnels. Above each tent entrance, one banner read, "American Red Cross" and another read, "FEMA Disaster Recovery Center."

The door to the bus opened again and a man in his late forties wearing a red vest and khaki pants stepped onto the bus.

"Okay, listen up, folks," he yelled.

Zach's classmates were audibly displeased with the situation, and their complaining grew louder as the man tried to gain order. Mr. Dean stood and held his arm over his head, his hand making a fist. It reminded Zach of his days in public elementary school assemblies.

The bus slowly quieted. When the noise was just a low mumbling, Mr. Dean spoke.

"All right, class. I know everyone's tired and we all just want to get home. But there's a procedure that has to be followed in a national emergency. We have to be patient and let these folks do their jobs. If everyone cooperates, we can get through this stage and be on our way home soon. So, everyone, quiet down and let the gentleman tell us what we need to do to get home."

Mr. Dean turned and gestured for the man to continue as he took his seat.

"In a moment, we'll have you exit the bus and proceed to the in-processing station. We'll be processing you in alphabetical order. There'll be three lines with one line for A-H and so on."

The man pointed to the first tent.

"We will need you to have your student identification card or driver's license ready if you have one. After you've filled out the registration forms, you'll be able to proceed to the check-in station. From there you will be directed to where you need to go next."

"When are we getting home? I have a date tonight," Connor yelled.

Everyone turned and laughed at him, prompting Mr. Dean to stand to get them to quiet down.

"The president has issued a shelter-in-place order, effective until further notice. Until we know what is going on, we'll need everyone to remain here. We will get you home as quickly as possible. But first, we must get through this process. Everyone, would you please stand and proceed in an orderly fashion to the front of the bus."

"What do you mean, shelter-in-place? What the hell does that mean?" someone yelled.

"No one is allowed to travel at the moment. We're doing our best to locate stranded motorists and provide shelter until the travel ban has been lifted," the man responded.

"What happened? Was it terrorists again?" another asked.

"Unfortunately, communications are down, and we don't have a lot of information right now. We do know that when it is safe to do so, the travel ban will be lifted, and we will get you all home to your parents. But right now, we just need a little cooperation while we get you settled here."

"Do we take our bags and stuff?" a girl asked.

"Bags?"

"Our backpacks and gym bags," she clarified.

"Yes, bring your things, but leave them outside the tent. They will need to be inspected before being allowed into the facility."

"Inspected? Why?" Jacob yelled.

Leaning close to Connor, Jacob said, "Man, you better stuff that weed down your pants."

Zach's heart sank. There was no way they would ever see their belongings again. Zach never went anywhere without his GHB— or get-home bag. He took his GHB to sleepovers, school, the dentist's office. He slept with it beside his bed. It was a part of him. There was no way in hell he was leaving it behind.

"It is to ensure everyone's safety. Now, if you will exit the bus, we will do our best to get you processed as quickly as possible and then on to the food tent. I am sure you all would like a nice hot meal by now."

Everyone on the bus stood and proceeded to the front. Zach hung back. He was desperately trying to form a plan. He went over all the scenarios he had trained for with his dad, but none of them fit the situation he now found himself in. He was screwed. He had let himself be taken behind enemy lines, and he couldn't think himself out of this one.

Zach was the last one to step off the bus. A mound of gym bags, backpacks, and handbags lay on the ground outside the tent. The thought struck him about how much money was lying there. While there were Nike or North Face brands, there were many more expensive bags in the pile. Most of his classmates came from wealthy families. Many were sons and daughter of doctors, lawyers, and business owners. Their parents could afford to replace the stuff heaped there. Most of it was useless to them now, anyway.

Zach's bag, however, was priceless to him. It contained all the things he needed to survive until he got home. The contents had been carefully chosen by his father. Each item had a purpose. There was nothing in the pack he was prepared to part with.

"This way, son," a woman in her late fifties said, pointing to the end of the line trailing out of the tent door. She wore a bright red shirt with American Red Cross and Disaster Relief written on it.

Zach held on to his pack, refusing to comply with the demand to leave it behind.

"You'll need to leave your bag here with the others," she said.

"I'm sorry, ma'am, but I can't leave my pack. It goes where I go. I don't mean any disrespect, but I'm not leaving it anywhere. You're welcome to inspect it, but I am not leaving it here."

The woman said something into her radio, and two armed men walked toward them. One wore a black, short-sleeve shirt with an IEMA logo on it, and the other was a Macon County Sheriff's deputy. Mr. Dean stepped outside the tent and rushed to Zach's side.

"Whoa, wait a minute. What is going on?" Mr. Dean demanded.

"Step back inside, sir. Let us handle this," the shorter of the two men said.

The taller man grabbed hold of Zach's pack while the other man took Zach by the arm. A third man arrived. This one had on a white polo shirt with lettering. Zach couldn't make out what it said. Zach's pack was handed to the white-polo-shirt guy. The deputy turned Zach around and pushed him onto the hood of a golf cart. Before Zach knew it, the man had his hands between Zach's legs patting him down. The officer pulled Zach's hands behind him and restrained his wrists with heavy police zip tie cuffs. Zach was shoved into the golf cart and taken to a hanger on the opposite end of the facility. As they drove away from the in-processing tent, Zach could tell they were in an airport. They had come in from the back, and the tent complex had obscured the runway. But looking back as they headed away from tents, Zach could see the traffic control tower and main terminal.

When they arrived at the hangar, the tall deputy pulled Zach from the golf cart by the arm and led him inside. A row of tables lined the far wall. Columns of folding chairs sat facing them. Zach was not the only one receiving a warm welcome.

Zach was shoved into a chair and told to sit and not say anything until he was called forward. He didn't know how they would call him forward since he hadn't given anyone his name yet. He thought Homeland Security had probably run facial recognition on him and already pulled up a detailed file of all his internet searches and Snapchat messages. Zach deduced that he was, indeed, fucked.

It took two-and-a-half hours before anyone called him forward. They didn't use his name. Someone had come by and handed him a number like his mom got when she went to the DMV to get her driver's license renewed.

An extremely thin woman who looked to be in her thirties called his number. Zach stood. He must have hesitated a bit too long, because a man with a beer belly that made him look nine months pregnant rushed over and nudged him forward. Zach nearly fell over the leather-clad biker in front of him, earning him the meanest stink-eye he'd ever seen.

The beer belly guy pushed on Zach's shoulder, causing him nearly to miss the chair as he sat down. The woman didn't look up. She continued writing something in a ledger like the ones used at polling places during elections—the ones his mom signed after giving them her ID and before receiving a ballot. Zach doubted they were conducting any elections at this place. He was quite sure that democracy was dead, evidenced by the illegal search and seizure of his property and his detainment for resisting.

"Name?"

The woman looked like she hated her job. She had so much disdain for the people she was charged with processing that she couldn't bring herself to extend the courtesy of looking at them.

Zach rapid-fired questions at the woman.

"What is this place? Why am I being held? I want my backpack."

"Name? I need your name."

"No, I'm not giving you my name until you answer my questions. I was brought here against my will. I just want my pack and I'll leave. I don't want your services. I can get home on my own."

The beer belly man was joined by a couple of black shirt goons, who proceeded to lead him through a door on the side of the hangar and into a small, windowless room. He heard the door lock from the outside as they left.

Things had gone from bad to worse.

The room was bare except for a bucket with a toilet seat attached. He'd seen one of those before. His dad had constructed one for his mom and sister to use when they primitive camped, at least in the early days. They had progressed to using the woods like he and his dad after a year or so. They preferred just using the woods over having the chore of cleaning the bucket. His dad's philosophy had been, if you used it, you cleaned it.

Zach sat on the concrete floor with his back against the wall, staring at the makeshift toilet. He did need to go, but he did not want to be trapped in the tiny room with that smell. He'd hold it as long as possible. Hopefully, he'd never have to use it.

CHAPTER 21

Red Cross Disaster Shelter
  Decatur Airport
  Decatur, Illinois

Time was hard to judge without daylight to gauge it. Zach tried to recall what time the bus had arrived to pick them up at the church. He figured they had arrived around ten o'clock that morning. Zach had watched the sunrise from his seat in the back of the church. The light had been beautiful streaming through the stained glass over the podium at the front of the sanctuary. Most churches had replaced stained glass with more efficient double-paned clear glass. That church must not have had that kind of budget.

They hadn't been provided lunch yet, so the bus had likely arrived before one o'clock that afternoon. They rode on the bus for about two or three hours, he guessed. He'd sat in the hangar for another two or three hours before he landed himself in solitary confinement. So, it was likely close to getting dark outside.

His stomach growled. He was dehydrated. He hadn't had anything to eat or drink since eight that morning.

Zach had never gone so long without food and water since he was eleven on one of his father's survival drills. That morning, Zach's dad had given him a minimal pack. He'd called it an every-day-carry, or EDC, pack. It contained only a small knife, a fire starter, a LifeStraw, a poncho, an emergency blanket, a compass, a flashlight, a couple of Band-Aids, energy powder, and three one-thousand-calorie energy bars. He'd provided Zach with grid coordinates and sent him to find a rally point where they would meet as a family later in the day.

Zach had messed up and missed the rally point by three miles. When he discovered that, he was hopelessly lost. He had sat down on a fallen log and waited for his dad to come find him. He was lost in the woods for two days.

The long, cold nights were worse than the hunger and thirst. He hated the dark and jumped at every rustling of leaves. By the time his dad had found him, he was exhausted, hungry, and dehydrated. His dad had been so cool about it. Zach had been afraid he'd yell at him, but he didn't. In fact, he said he had gotten lost the first time he set out on his own too. He had been in basic training, though, and his squad had found him pretty quickly. Zach's mom had been the one to yell. She yelled at Zach and gave dirty looks to his dad the rest of the trip home.

A tapping noise brought Zach back into the present. It was coming from the other side of the wall he was leaning against. The tapping sound moved up and down and side to side.

Is someone testing the wall for studs?

He'd seen Ryan do that before when they were doing some remodeling for his mom and had ripped out the wall between their dining room and the kitchen—before his mom had met Jason, and before they'd sold the house. Ryan had given Zach a dirty look when Zach had handed him his dad's stud finder.

Zach rapped on the wall with his knuckles. Three quick raps, then three slow, then three more fast. Three fast, three slow, and three more fast was the response from the other side of the wall. It was his friend, Connor. They had used that code when they were younger and they'd had sleepovers in Zach's treehouse. It was Morse code for "SOS."

"Connor, is that you?"

"Zach? It's me. Dude, what the hell is going on?"

"I'm not sure. I refused to answer their stupid questions. How did you end up here?"

"I asked too many questions, I guess."

"What happened with the others? Did you see where they took them?" Zach asked.

He waited for his friend's reply, but none came. He heard banging and the sounds of a struggle and then a door being slammed.

"Connor? Connor?" Zach yelled to the wall.

After a few minutes, the door opened and two men in black rushed in. They grabbed Zach and dragged him from the room. Fear made Zach compliant. He knew that, at that moment, there was nothing he could do, and resisting would only get him hurt. There were too many of them, and he was defenseless against them.

Zach was taken to an in-processing unit with at least ten armed guards. Zach gave the person behind the desk his name, his parents' names, and his grandparents' names, along with their addresses. Funny, they didn't ask for any of their phone numbers. Zach didn't tell them about his sister. By doing so, he hoped he was protecting her.

A white plastic bracelet like the ones used in hospitals was placed on his left wrist and right ankle. They were stamped with numbers and a bar code.

Am I now just a number?

From the in-processing unit, he was taken to a holding tent. He was issued new clothes in a lovely shade of gray and a pair of men's sandals, also gray. Another unfriendly woman handed him two pairs of white briefs, size large, and two pairs of white crew-length socks. She pointed to the next station. Zach went and stood in that line, clutching his new possessions to his chest.

He was handed a bedroll, toiletries, and a bag for his clothes. He suddenly felt that he was on an episode of some prison show.

Zach followed the man in front of him through a door into a large space with at least thirty cots lined up in neat rows. Men and boys were busy making their cots and dressing in their new wardrobes. There was no privacy. Guards looked on as the occupants undressed and donned the uniforms. Zach felt self-conscious, but after setting his bedroll on his cot, he changed into his dull garb.

It was dark outside by the time food was brought in. Each person was given a tray containing some kind of stew, crackers, and a bottle of water. Zach considered hiding his spoon to make a shank. He had heard they could be fashioned into effective weapons, but he thought better of it after one of the guards stared at him a little too long.

The stew was tasteless but filling. Zach most appreciated the water. He felt so dehydrated that he could have downed half a dozen and still felt parched. He thought it unlikely they would provide them with more than one at a time. They would probably only get them with their meals. Forty-eight ounces of water a day was enough to survive, but not enough to be healthy. Maybe there would be a drinking fountain or something when they allowed them out of the tents. If they ever did.

Zach looked around but didn't see Connor or anyone from his class. He wondered if there were other tents like this one—tents for the troublemakers. Or was this the way they were treating all their guests?

Zach sat on his cot and stared around the tent. The blank faces of those around him told the tale of journeys similar to Zach's.

Most looked like they had given up and decided to go along to get along. Zach wasn't about to give up. He'd watch and wait. He'd wait for an opportune time to escape the camp and head home.

Without his gear, a 100-mile trip would be extremely difficult. But he wouldn't let that stop him. And if he could, he'd try to help his friends and Mr. D.

Lights-out came shortly after the dinner trays had been collected. His captors did make sure they collected every plastic spoon. Once the lights were out, the men in black left. Zach was sure they would stand guard just outside the exits, though he resisted the urge to sneak over and find out. Causing trouble might get him thrown back into solitary, and he'd lose his chance to escape.

"Hey, were you with the bus of kids from the church?" a voice spoke in the darkness.

"Yeah. Do you know where they took my classmates? Did they leave already?" Zach said.

"No, they are still here. No one leaves."

"What?"

"They tell everyone that they are going to help them get home. But buses come in loaded with people and leave empty. No one has left since I got here yesterday afternoon."

"That is what I was afraid of. I heard about camps like this before the shit hit the fan."

"You one of those conspiracy nuts always talking about the end of the world?" the voice asked.

"Not so nutty sounding now, is it?" Zach asked.

"No, I guess not. I may have to apologize to my brother-in-law —if I ever see him again, that is."

"You and everyone else who has prepper family members, probably."

"If he's right, they already rounded him up and locked him away in a camp like this one—or worse."

"Where are you from?" Zach asked.

"I'm from Vegas, but my sister and brother-in-law live in Oklahoma."

"Were you traveling alone?"

"No, I got my boy with me. I am grateful they didn't split us up like they did some families."

"They split up families?"

"Yeah. Women are in one tent and kids are being kept on the opposite side of the camp near the hangars. Men are in the middle, like us. I am not sure why they allow those of us in here to keep our sons with us."

"Yeah, if they split up other families, it doesn't make sense for them to allow the troublemaker tent to keep their kids."

"What makes you think this is the troublemaker tent?' the man asked.

"Because I'm in here."

The man laughed.

"I'm Zach. What is your name?"

"James."

"Well, James, what is your theory on what they have planned for our group?"

A flashlight flicked on at the opposite end of the tent. A man walked up and down the aisles between the cots, shining the light in each person's face. Zach rolled over and covered his face with this arm, pretending to be asleep. He heard the cot next to him squeak and assumed James had done the same.

Zach heard the guard shuffle past him and let out the breath he had held. He peeked under his arm and watched the light disappear at the other end of the tent.

"It really is like a prison—bed checks and all."

"I think you may be right, Zach. I think we're about to discover that we're no longer free citizens of the United States of America."

CHAPTER 22

Grundy, County, Illinois
Event + 2 days

Carl and Kelly made their way back to the old farmhouse where Carl had seen the injured girl. They stalked around the house, looking for a good entry point. Just as Carl rounded the back corner, a boy bounded from the house with a shotgun under his arm. Carl jumped back just before being spotted, bumping into Kelly and knocking him down.

Grabbing Kelly by the shirt, Carl pulled him to his feet and shoved him backward.

"They have guns," Carl whispered.

"I don't want to shoot no kid, Carl. You said these were just for show. I ain't shooting nobody." Kelly held his pistol out and shoved it into his brother's chest.

"Don't point that at me!" Carl said, pushing Kelly's gun to the side. "Get a fucking grip, Kelly. We don't have to shoot nobody. We have to make sure they don't shoot us, though."

"How we gonna do that? We run up in there pointing guns,

they gonna shoot at us, and we'll have to shoot back. I ain't agreed to that, Carl."

"Bro, we ain't gonna run up in there, guns all-a-blazing. We're waiting for them to come out, and we'll take them one at a time, starting with the boy there."

Carl pointed in the direction the boy ran. Kelly peeked around the corner of the house.

"Looks like he's fixing to go hunting or something. He's putting gas in that wheeler back by the barn."

"Okay, let's just wait until he leaves then. One less gun to deal with, you see," Carl said with a wide smile.

The brothers listened as the four-wheeler's engine started. The men backed up and made their way back to the tree line as the boy drove past them down the driveway and out of sight.

Carl sprinted across to the corner of the house, Kelly close behind. Carl stopped and peeked around the house into the back yard. Not detecting any movement, he crouched moved under a window, stopping at the other side. He pushed his back against the house and motioned for his brother to stay where he was.

Carl leaned forward and peered into the window. A middle-aged woman was changing sheets on the bed. He couldn't see the girls.

Carl motioned for his brother to crouch low and move forward. Kelly followed his brother to the back door. Carl leapt over the steps and pressed his back against the house on the other side of the door. Kelly stayed on the opposite side. Carl peeked through the open door. There she was. She was even more beautiful than he had imagined. Her long, lean body moved gracefully as she went about her business, unaware of the two men outside.

Carl smiled broadly and pointed to the door. Kelly mouthed, "She in there?"

Carl nodded, then burst into the kitchen, gun pointed at the girl. She let out a scream before Kelly grabbed her and put his hand over her mouth. Her eyes went wide as she clawed at his grasp. Carl walked over and stroked her long, blonde hair.

Placing his face into a handful of her hair, Carl sniffed deeply. He exhaled out slowly, eyes closed. Pity he had to sell her. He'd like to take her with them and set up house in a new town.

The girl stomped on Kelly's foot. He bent over, hitting his mouth on her shoulder. He hopped on one foot as he tried to maintain his hold while keeping his hand over her mouth.

Carl leaned in close to her ear.

"Listen up, girl. You better calm down and be nice or we might just have to hurt the old lady and that little girl."

The girl's eyes widened, then filled with tears. She stopped struggling in Kelly's grip.

"That's better. You be good and nobody is going to get hurt here today. Got that?"

The girl nodded.

"Let's go, Kelly."

Carl opened the door, and Kelly pushed the girl forward while still maintaining his grip on her mouth. Just as Carl turned to go out, he heard a shotgun rack. Carl swung around. Kelly released the girl and turned. It happened in slow motion.

Kelly threw his hands up, and the pistol in his right hand clattered to the floor. The girl dropped to a crouch as the boom of the shotgun shattered the window to Carl's right. Carl ducked down and fired, hitting the woman. He continued to fire as she fell, her shotgun clattering to the floor.

Kelly stumbled back and pressed himself against the wall, his eyes never leaving the bleeding woman. The girl screamed and tried to go to the woman, but Carl caught her by her hair. He yanked her back toward him, causing her to lose her balance and fall to the floor. He pressed the pistol hard against her head.

"Kelly, grab that shotgun," Carl yelled.

"Who else is here? Anyone else gonna come try to shoot me this morning?"

"No. It is just us," the girl said.

"You best be telling me the truth, girly. As you can see, I ain't in a playing mood. I don't appreciate some old bag shooting at me before I even had my breakfast."

"What do you want? I don't have any money, and I don't think they have any either, but—"

"Where's the money at?"

"I don't know where she keeps her purse."

"Kelly," Carl yelled at his brother. "Kelly!"

Kelly stared at the woman on the floor, then back to Carl, his expression blank.

"Snap the fuck out of it. We have work to do, bro. Pick up the shotty and go search the place. Find me the woman's bag. I imagine that is where we'll find her cash."

Kelly looked back at the woman, then at the door she had come through, but he didn't move.

"Move it, Kelly! Move your fucking ass!" Carl yelled, spittle flying from his lips.

Kelly crept around the dying woman's body. He stopped and looked down at her. He slowly reached down and picked up the shotgun. He stared at the blood-spattered gun.

"I'm sorry," Kelly said, darting out of the kitchen and down a hall.

Carl dragged Maddie over to a stool by the kitchen island and pushed her onto it.

"Sit there and be good. As soon as we grab the money, we will get out of here."

"Yes, just take the money and go," she said, brushing hair from her face.

"Oh, we will, but you're coming with us. We have someone we would like you to meet. It's your lucky day. He's gonna give you a job."

"No, I'm not going. You can kill me—"

Carl reached out and slapped her hard across the face.

She reached up with her left hand and covered the red mark on her face. She glared back at Carl, her hazel eyes blazing into him.

"I ain't going nowhere with you freaks."

Carl yanked her to the floor by her hair and put his foot on her neck. He pressed the muzzle of the pistol to her forehead.

"Do it. Just do it now. You will have to kill me, cause I ain't leaving here with you."

"Kelly, get the fuck in here," Carl yelled, pressing the pistol harder against her head.

Kelly ran into the room and stopped at the body of the woman.

"Get the fuck over here, you pussy. Help me tie this bitch up before I have to blow her fucking brains out. Mouthy-ass bitch is pissing me off," Carl said, the veins in his forehead popping as his face turned deep red.

Kelly stepped over the woman and retrieved a bag of zip ties from his back pocket. Carl grabbed the girl by her hair, shoving the pistol into her abdomen.

"I hear being gut-shot hurts like a motherfucker. How about I shoot you and let you bleed out like your momma over there?" Carl said as he spun her around backwards on the stool.

She didn't resist. Kelly grabbed the girl's wrists, wrapped the zip ties around them, and pulled them tight.

"Get her feet too."

Kelly did as instructed and zip-tied her feet together. They left her on her stomach in the kitchen as they ransacked the house. Carl heard the motor of the four-wheeler through the open front bedroom window and ran to tell Kelly.

Carl ran from the woman's bedroom just in time to see the boy barreling down the drive, the shotgun across his lap.

"Go shut the back door. When he opens it, we'll shoot him," Carl said, pointing toward the back.

"Fuck no, I ain't shooting no boy. There weren't supposed to be no shooting. This is fucked up. I didn't sign up for this shit."

Kelly paced the room, waving his arms over his head.

"All right, you little whiny baby. We won't shoot the boy. We'll just invite him to have a seat next to his dead momma."

"I ain't hurting no kid. And neither are you. We tie him up like the girl there. Ain't no need to hurt him. We just leave him here and take the girl. No one else needs to get hurt. You hear me, Carl?"

"You're starting to really piss me off, brother, but all right. You grab the kid and tie him up, and we'll leave him like you said. If it goes sideways and I have to shoot him, it is on you," Carl said, pointing at his brother.

Kelly shook his head and ran to the kitchen. He sidestepped the body on the floor and quietly shut the back door just as he heard the engine of the four-wheeler die.

Carl tapped his thigh with his fingertips as they waited for the boy to open the door. They heard him coming. He was whistling some tune Carl didn't recognize. He motioned for Kelly to stand beside the door while he ducked into the breakfast nook out of sight.

When the door opened, the boy immediately froze. Instead of running to his mother's side, as Carl expected he'd do, the boy turned and started down the steps. He was halfway back to the ATV when Carl leveled his pistol and shot him in the back.

"Fuck, Carl, what did you do?" Kelly said, pounding his fists against the counter and kicking over a trash can.

"He'd have ran next door and brought back a bunch of cousins and shit. I couldn't risk that. You want to get shot in the back by some camo-wearing bubba while we try to get to our wheeler with the girl?"

"I don't know why I let you talk me into this shit," Kelly said, crouching to the floor and putting his head between his knees. "I said I don't want to be a part of no killing, and you go and shoot a kid in the fucking back."

"We ain't got time to stand around here arguing about it now.

We gotta get the hell out of here before someone comes looking to see what the shooting was all about."

Carl shoved Kelly toward the open door.

"Now you go get the boy's wheeler and bring it up here. We'll throw the girl in it and get the hell out of here."

Before descending the steps, Kelly looked over his shoulder at the girl.

A moment later, Kelly pulled the four-wheeler up the steps and parked it, motor running. Grabbing the girl by her arms, Carl motioned for Kelly to grab her feet and help him carry her down the steps. As she struggled in their grasp, her head banged against the door frame, causing her to cry out.

"Damn it, Kelly. Be careful. Boss ain't gonna pay top dollar for her all banged up. It is bad enough she's got that scrape on her cheek and a fat lip."

"Sorry."

Once out the door, the girl began to scream at the top of her lungs. Carl put a hand over her mouth as they shoved her down hard onto the trailer.

"Get me something to stuff in her mouth. We need to shut this bitch up before someone hears her."

After running into the house, Kelly returned with a handful of dishtowels. Carl stuffed one in the girl's mouth. After tying two towels together, he tied the towels around her head to hold the gag in place.

"Jump in and I'll drop you off at our wheeler," Carl said, pointing to the trailer.

Kelly jumped in, bumping into the girl as Carl floored it away from the house, throwing gravel behind them.

CHAPTER 23

Minooka, Illinois
  Event, + 2 days

Maddie squirmed and tried to roll onto her back, but there wasn't sufficient room with the man nearly sitting on top of her. The plastic ties cut into her wrists as she struggled. She wiggled and rubbed her face on her shoulder, attempting to dislodge the dishtowel tied around her head.

By the sound of gravel under the tires, she could tell they were on the I&M Canal Trail. Maddie lay still, listening for sounds to give her an indication on which way they were going. They hadn't traveled all that far before the four-wheeler came to an abrupt stop, causing Maddie to slide forward and hit her head on the trailer. The man who rode in the back with her grabbed her by one arm and dragged her out. Maddie landed on the ground on her side, her shoulder striking concrete. The second man placed his hands under her arms, and the man with her grabbed her feet. The two men carried her up a short flight of steps and through a door into a dark space. Maddie was tossed onto a mattress on the floor.

After rolling over as far from the men as possible, Maddie attempted to sit up. The plastic ties cut deeper into her wrists as she tried to push herself up. Exhausted from her struggle, Maddie lay on her back, trying to get enough air.

The space was dark and musky. The only light shined through a slit in the door.

"I'm just gonna sit here a minute and have a smoke," one man said.

Maddie couldn't see his face in the dark, but she believed him to be the man who had shot Darlene and Ray Junior. An image of poor Ray Junior face-first on the ground, shot in the back, caused bile to rise in her throat. Her mind began to race. She had been taken by animals. Men who would shoot women and children. She couldn't comprehend what their intentions for her were, but their willingness to kill so brutally convinced her that her own chances of survival were thin.

After a while, Maddie could hear both men snoring softly. Sitting on the mattress on the floor of the dark and musky room, she could barely make out a figure lying on the sofa about six feet away. She looked around the room where the other man was sleeping in a chair. The room was small, maybe eight-by-ten. It opened into an even smaller kitchen. A hall ran off the kitchen. A door that Maddie thought to be a front exit door was to her left. What was possibly a bedroom door was on the wall across from the front door. It was similar to a camping trailer. Maybe a small trailer home.

She attempted to sit up straight but found it difficult to do with her hands behind her back. She laid down and tried to slip her zip-tied hands under her buttocks to bring them to the front, but her hands were too painful from the fall and the zip ties cut into her wrist. She rolled onto her side and pushed herself up. She surveyed the room. It stank like piss, puke, cigarettes, and body odor. Very strong body odor.

She had to pee so bad. She wasn't sure she could hold it. She did not want to pee herself, but she sure the hell didn't want to wake the creeps across the room. She needed to find a back door and get the hell out of there. She scooted off the mattress onto the floor. Peering around a half-wall into the kitchen, Maddie looked down the hall and could see what looked to be a back door.

Maddie tried to push herself to her feet and stumbled, knocking over a small table. The man in the chair stirred. Maddie sat frozen in place, willing the man to go back to sleep.

He did not. Instead, he sat up straight.

"Carl?"

Carl didn't answer.

"Carl, is that you?" the man asked.

Kelly stood and walked over to the mattress before spotting Maddie near the kitchen.

"What're you doing?" he asked, rushing over to her. He bent down and grabbed her arm. "You trying to get yourself killed?"

Maddie struggled against the man's grasp, but she couldn't get enough traction to pull away.

"If he wakes up and catches you trying to get away, he will hurt you, stupid girl."

Kelly dragged Maddie back to the mattress and gently lay her on her side.

Maddie tried to tell him that she just needed to pee, but with the gag in her mouth, he couldn't understand her. After the fourth attempt, he appeared to understand.

"Oh, you need to pee. Um—the water ain't working and the toilet is pretty rank in there, but if you behave, I'll let you go pee."

Maddie nodded in agreement. Kelly pulled a knife from his pocket and unfolded it. She gasped.

"I'm gonna cut the restraints on your feet."

He slid the knife under the ties and freed her feet. It felt wonderful to not have the zip ties gouging into the skin of her sore ankle. She had high hopes that he'd untie her hands. The bathroom was likely down the hall near the back door. She could bolt out the door and get away before he could even grab her. That was her hope anyway.

"I ain't gonna cut the ones on your hands—Carl would kill me if I did that—so you best behave while I take you to the bathroom or else it won't be very pretty for you."

Grabbing her arm, Kelly pulled her to her feet. He led her through the tiny kitchen. Dirty dishes filled the sink and lined the counters. Maddie stumbled over takeout containers and pizza boxes. The contents of the trash can overflowed onto the floor. It smelled so bad it made Maddie gag.

"You think that stinks, you just wait until you lift the lid to the shitter. I can't stand it, so I just go outside."

Maddie couldn't believe the smell. It hit her as soon as Kelly opened the door to the bathroom. She felt as if she were going to vomit and feared she'd gag on it if she did. As she fought back the urge, Kelly reached up and pulled down her gag.

Immediately, Maddie spewed vomit into the bathtub. Finished retching, she held her hands out from her back, gesturing for Kelly to remove her hand restraints. Kelly shook his head no.

"How am I supposed to pull my pants down?"

Kelly looked down at her jeans then looked back up.

"No. You aren't undressing me," Maddie said sternly.

Kelly pulled out his knife, and Maddie turned around. Once he had cut the restraints, Kelly stepped out into the hall and shut the door.

Maddie opted not to open the lid to the toilet, instead squatting over the tub. After relieving herself, she looked around the dark bathroom for something to use as a weapon. Scissors, fingernail file, even a toilet brush or plunger would at least be something, but there was nothing.

A small rap at the door stopped her search.

"You done in there?"

The door cracked open, and Maddie stepped out. The back door was just across from the bathroom. She'd wait until both men were asleep and would sneak out that door. She just needed to be patient.

Kelly lead Maddie back to the mattress and zip-tied her hands, this time in front of her. Maddie scooted back and sat cross-legged. Her wrist hurt where the restraints had cut into her skin.

"Are you brothers?" Maddie asked.

"Yeah."

"You younger or older?"

"Younger," he said.

"I have a younger brother. He can be a pain in the ass most of the time, but he's my brother, so it's okay."

Kelly said nothing.

"He's fourteen, but he thinks he's grown or something. When my dad died, he got all man-of-the-house attitude and tried to boss me around and shit."

"Yeah, Carl bosses me around a lot. It can get annoying."

"Zach would be all like, you shouldn't be hanging with those people, or you missed curfew again. I'd remind him that I used to change his diapers and that he wasn't Dad."

Maddie remembered that conversation like it was yesterday. That was not all she had said. She had been angry with Zach for calling her out on missing curfew. She had told him he was not her father—that he was nothing like their dad and never would be. The pained look on his face still haunted her. She wished now that she had apologized to him. She wished she had told him how much he was like dad. He looked like him. His mannerisms were like him. He had the same you're-in-deep-shit tone when he scolded her. That was what she had been angry about. He reminded her too much of their dad, and it had made her miss him too much.

"Where is your brother?" Kelly asked.

"He was on a class field trip when this shit happened. He's somewhere in southern Illinois with his class."

"At least he isn't alone. There are teachers with him, right?"

"Yeah. All but one will be useless in this shit. But Mr. Dean—

he was in the military. He has seen some shit. He knows how to handle himself. I trust him to take care of Zach. The rest of them, well, I feel sorry for Mr. Dean having to deal with their whiny asses."

Kelly laughed.

Carl coughed and moaned. He rolled back and forth on the sofa but didn't wake.

"Bad dreams?"

"No, he's detoxing. He does that if he doesn't shoot up every four-to-six hours. That shit is getting impossible to get right now."

"Oh, that sucks, I guess," Maddie said. "Do you use too?"

"Nah, I hate that shit. I've watched it destroy everyone I love."

"I can see why you hate it."

"How did your dad die?" Kelly asked.

Maddie was quiet. She didn't want to discuss such a painful subject with this low-life piece of shit, but her strategy to win him over and convince him to let her go might require she put that aside. She exhaled slowly and looked at her feet. She could barely see them in the dark.

"He was killed by a drunk driver."

"That blows."

"Yep."

"How old were you?"

"Fifteen."

Maddie leaned forward. The restraints dug into her wrists, but she needed to sit up straight to catch her breath. She wiggled her way back and pressed herself against the wall. Her shoulder burned. She tried to focus on the pain in her wrist and shoulders, focusing on anything but the pain in her heart. She never talked about that day. Her heart pounded in her chest. She felt bile rise again in her throat. But talking about losing her dad might just save her life.

No pain. No gain.

A single tear dripped from the corner of her eye. In the darkness, her captor couldn't see it. She made no attempt to wipe it away. She would honor her dad with them. To be weak now in this situation was to be strong.

How ironic.

"He went out to get ice for our cooler. I was going to run my first fifty-K the next day. He had run with me that morning and helped me get ready for the race. After an hour, when he hadn't made it home from the convenience store around the block, I knew something had happened."

"That really sucks. My dad is in prison. He's never helped me with shit. My grandma and grandpa were the ones to raise me and Carl—until my mom came home, that is. Life went to shit for me after that."

"But at least you had grandparents who cared for you?"

"My grandma did, but she died. My grandpa did until my mom came home. He judges me because of how my mom and brother act."

Carl's groaning increased and grew louder. He rolled from side to side.

"He's gonna wake up soon. He'll be really grumpy and mean until he gets his fix. I should go and see if I can score some before he wakes up."

"Why?"

"Why? He's my brother, and he's sick. He can't help that he's a junkie. He didn't have much choice with my mom like she was."

"But you aren't a junkie and you lived the same life, right?"

"It was different for me."

"You could just go. You could release me, and we could go together. You could get away from all these drugs and violence. You'd have a chance to make a better life for yourself."

"I can't leave my brother. We don't throw away family."

"Don't you ever want a family of your own? Do you want to literally be your brother's keeper the rest of your life?"

"I'm not my brother's keeper. He takes care of me. He has all my life," Kelly said, his voice raised.

Maddie knew she was pushing him too hard, but she was desperate. She had to risk it. He may be her only hope to get out of there.

"I don't deserve this, Kelly. I've done nothing to you or Carl to deserve this. I have a family that loves me, and I love them. I just want to get home to my mom and my little brother. Can't you please help me?"

Kelly said nothing.

"Please? Just let me go. You don't have to worry about the police. I haven't even seen one since the lights went out. I won't tell anyone." Maddie scooted to the end of the mattress and leaned closer to Kelly

"Please, Kelly?"

"I can't. Carl will kill me if I do. I just can't. He's my brother, and I won't betray him. He's all I have in the world."

A sudden rush of anger washed over Maddie. It shocked her. She expected that she'd feel sad and defeated by his refusal, but all she felt was rage. These two pieces of shit stood between her and getting home. She could not give up and let the men turn her over to even worse people. She scooted back on the mattress and lay on her side. She needed another plan. She couldn't let these two win.

She would not.

CHAPTER 24

Minooka, Illinois
Event + 3 days

When the second man awoke, Maddie's patience was wearing thin. The man stretched, yawned, and scratched at his groin.

"Kelly, where's my shit?"

"You used it all yesterday. You've been asleep for over twelve hours."

"Shit, why the hell did you let me sleep that long?"

"I couldn't wake you up, Carl. I tried, but you shot too much of that shit. I thought I'd lost you there for a while."

Standing, the man stretched and then spewed vomit all over the floor. Maddie pulled her feet back just in time.

After laying back down, the man rubbed his head and rocked back and forth on the sofa. He moaned softly.

"I need you to go see Jimmy again, Kelly. I need a little something so we can get this bitch up to the boss and get paid. I can get some H from Junior after I get paid."

"You mean when we get paid?"

Kelly stood and walked toward the door.

"Yeah, I mean we. Now just get me some shit, all right? I'm hurting bad here."

Waving over his shoulder, Kelly shut the door behind him. Maddie began to tremble. She had been left alone with a killer. She had witnessed him kill two people the day before, and she had no doubt that he'd kill her if she pissed him off or tried to get away.

Sitting up, the man popped something into his mouth, took a sip from a glass on a side table, and lay back on the sofa. Within minutes, the man was snoring. Maddie had her chance. It was now or never.

Maddie slid to the end of the mattress and pushed herself up. At least Kelly hadn't put the restraints back on her feet. She needed to find something to cut the ties off her hands, but rummaging around in the dark might wake the man.

Tiptoeing into the kitchen, Maddie looked through the mass of dirty dishes on the counter for something sharp enough to cut through the plastic. There wasn't anything but butter knives. As she tugged gently on the top drawer, it squeaked loudly. She froze. Maddie turned her head. The man stirred on the sofa.

Maddie crouched down and made her way to the back door. Her whole body shook as she reached up and felt around for the handle. Feeling the cold metal in her hand, Maddie turned the knob. She gently pulled on it. The door didn't budge. She pulled a little harder and nothing happened.

The door opens out.

She pushed, but the door didn't open. She pushed harder. It didn't budge. She heard a crash in the living room. The man came barreling through the kitchen. Maddie felt the hard, cold steel of the gun pressed against her cheek.

"I just needed to pee. I'm sorry I woke you. I'm sorry," Maddie cried.

"Get the fuck back in there and stop whining."

Pulling her by her hair, Carl led her through the kitchen. With a shove, he threw her onto the smelly mattress.

"You just sit tight there, bitch. When my brother gets back, we're going to take you up to meet some real nice friends of mine. Until then, you just sit there and be quiet, you hear?"

Not much light shined into the room except through a small window in the door. No light at all came through the windows.

After taking a seat back onto the sofa, Carl leaned back, lit a joint, and closed his eyes. The gun lay in his lap. Maddie stared at it. She was trapped. Her hope to escape through the back door now dashed, she laid back on the mattress and wept quietly.

She thought of poor Emma, alone in Darlene's house. How traumatized she must be after witnessing her parents being brutally killed, then seeing what happened to Darlene and Ray Junior. What hope did she have to survive now, on her own in this crazy world? Maddie could not help her now. She couldn't protect herself, let alone a ten-year-old girl. Maybe it was better to die at the beginning of the apocalypse than slowly starve to death later, anyway. Maddie was not as afraid of death as she was of living in her present situation. There were some things worse than death, and this was one of them.

As scared as she was, Maddie was also totally exhausted and eventually fell asleep. Something ran across her foot, startling her awake. She sat up and pulled her feet under her. The room was pitch black.

It must be night. How long was I out?

Sitting on the mattress with her back against the wall, Maddie stared in the direction of the man. She heard his snores and moans. He sounded like he was in terrible pain. She hoped he would die. That realization bothered her. What kind of person was she becoming? She'd seen so much violence and death over the last few days.

Had it been days? She wasn't even sure.

She tried to remember what day it was. She had spent the first night, after the lights went out, hiding behind a shed with the

Andrews family. The second night, she and Emma had stayed in the cemetery. The next day, she and Emma had hit the trail and met Darlene and Ray Junior. That memory brought a flood of tears. Slumping down the wall, Maddie lay on her side in a fetal position and let the river of tears flow. She didn't even try to stop them.

She cried for Darlene. She cried for poor little Ray Junior walking in and seeing his mother on the floor in a pool of blood only to be shot down in his own back yard. He was supposed to be safe there. But he wasn't safe in his home. Maybe no one was safe anywhere now.

The world was becoming just what her dad had said it would when the shit hit the fan. And he was not there to save her. No one was coming to save her. She was alone. She was on her own, and that scared her more than death.

Morning came and Kelly still hadn't returned. The light shined brighter and brighter through the window of the door, and the man on the sofa continued to moan and restlessly roll around.

Maddie could tell that the man was sick or something. Sweat dripped off his face, and he shook like he was freezing. He clutched his stomach and had vomited several times. The gun still lay next to him. No matter how weak or sick he was, he likely could still shoot her if she tried to get to the door and flee.

Her stomach began growling loudly. She wished she still had her pack. She remembered the wonderful rabbit soup Darlene had given her. She remembered warming soup on her rocket stove on hiking trips with her dad.

When she was younger, her dad would load the family up in his Jeep and go to some remote wilderness in southern Missouri. They would hike until dark. When they would complain about the weight of the packs or the pace of the hike, her dad would say that someday they'd be glad to know what they were capable of doing.

When they arrived at a suitable campsite, her dad would teach them a new way to build an emergency shelter. He taught them how to conceal their campsite and how to get away if they were discovered. They purified water using their LifeStraws and even learned to filter water through sand and a sock.

At her dad's hunting cabin, he had taught them the four rules of gun safety, how to shoot at moving targets, and how to disassemble and clean every gun he owned—and he owned a lot of them. Maddie looked at the man's gun. It looked like the Glock G42 she'd picked up from the man in the street. She doubted that the gangster had cleaned it regularly, and Carl hadn't cleaned it after he had used it to kill Darlene and Ray Junior.

That memory brought a new round of tears.

Harden the fuck up, Maddie. This shit ain't gonna get you home.

She stared at the gun lying next to the man. She tried to imagine what her dad would have done in this situation. She regretted that she hadn't taken his lessons seriously when all he was doing was trying to give her the skills to save her life. She had been an ungrateful brat. She felt such guilt that she had distanced herself from him during the year before the accident. She had let others' opinions of her dad influence hers. How disappointed he must have been with her.

He had been proud of her accomplishments in school and in her cross-country races. He quit pushing her to go to the cabin and do drills, but it must have pained him for her to pull away from him like she had. She tried to remember the last time she had gone to the cabin with him.

Was it the summer before my freshman year in high school?

Some of her dad's friends from the military had joined them. Uncle Ryan had been there. He had shown her and Zach how to tie ten different types of knots. He had also shown them how to get out of someone's grip if grabbed by the arm. Suddenly, a light bulb went on in her head. She could recall, vividly, how he had demonstrated how to break zip ties.

Maddie looked over at the man. She took a deep breath. She had to do this now. She needed to make her move before the other brother came back. Once they were both there, she didn't think she could take them both. It was now or never.

Sitting up straight, Maddie raised her hands high in the air above her head. She kept her eyes on the man, looking for any movement. Bringing her hands down in one rapid movement, she chicken winged her elbows, pushing down hard across her waist and using her abdomen as a wedge, simultaneously spreading her hands out as far as possible.

Shit!

It hurt like hell, and her wrists were bleeding now, but she tried again and again. The plastic zip ties refused to break. She had been able to break them every time when she had practiced with Uncle Ryan. Of course, she hadn't been dehydrated and her wrists hadn't been already cut up. Maddie took a deep breath and exhaled. She looked over to Carl. He rolled and coughed but didn't wake.

She wasn't going to have the strength to break them. She needed to use a friction saw. She was so glad she had continued to replace all her shoelaces with paracord. Really, swapping them out had been more of a habit. Every time they bought new shoes, her dad would have them remove the laces and use paracord instead.

Maddie reached down and untied her left shoe. She pulled the paracord from the shoe and laid it between her feet. She was out of practice, so tying the first bowline knot took more time than she would have liked. She was sweating profusely now. She had to keep reminding herself to breathe. The man could wake up at any moment or the brother could return. Any number of other bad things could occur that could stop her from getting away. She had to get this right, and she had to be quick about it.

Using her teeth, she pulled the second knot tight. Sliding the loop over the toe of her right shoe, Maddie slid it down to the middle of her foot. She fished the opposite end of the cord through the zip tie, then down to her left shoe. Looping the other end over her shoe, she extended her legs in front of her, pulling the cord tight. Making a bicycle motion with her legs, Maddie moved her legs back and forth. The friction of the paracord on the plastic of the zip tie made a squeaking noise. She stopped and put her feet down, watching for any movement from the man.

When he didn't stir, she lifted her legs and continued her bicycle motions for another twenty seconds and the tie broke. Her hands were free. Slipping the paracord off, Maddie untied the knots and quickly put the paracord back in her shoes. With her shoes laced tight, she slowly stood from the mattress, never taking her eyes from the man. As she started to take her first step, Carl sat up.

"Where the hell do you think you're going?" Carl said, rising to his feet.

Maddie sprinted for the door, but she tripped on a pile of shoes and fell against the wall. She shot to her feet and tried to reach the door before Carl could grab her, but he was on her before she got her hand to the knob.

Maddie swung around and punched him in the face. He stumbled back a step but didn't release his grip on her hair. She kicked sideways, hitting him in the knee. Carl yelped and let go, but he was quickly back on her. He pulled on her arm and she pushed into him, causing both to crash to the floor. She landed on top of Carl, then rolled off the stunned man and leapt to her feet. She stepped back and her foot hit something hard and metallic.

The gun!

She scrambled for the weapon, scooped it up, and was bringing it up into a firing position as the front door opened, flooding the room with light. Carl turned to look toward open door. Without hesitating, Maddie leveled the pistol at him and fired two rounds, both hitting center mass.

"No!" Kelly yelled as he stepped inside.

He raced to his brother's side, dropping to his knees.

"I'm sorry," Maddie said, looking down at the two men.

"You bitch. You shot my brother," Kelly snarled.

Maddie stepped sideways toward the door, the pistol raised and pointed at Kelly.

"I'm sorry. I had no choice. You should have let me go."

"You fucking bitch. You killed my brother," Kelly said, standing and taking a step toward her.

"Stop!" Maddie yelled. "Stop. Don't come any closer. I am going to leave now. There's no need for you to die too."

"He was all I had left in the world, and you took him from me."

Kelly kept walking.

Pop! Pop!

Two shots hit Kelly center mass, and he fell next to his brother on the floor. His eyes were open—a look of shock was on his face. Maddie froze in place, staring at the two men.

"Run, Maddie!" she heard her dad yell.

And she did.

Still gripping the pistol in her right hand, she ran down the steps and around the trailer. She didn't stop running until she reached a wooded area outside of town. She dropped to her knees on a soft bed of leaves and wept. She rocked back and forth, holding her head in her hands. Her ears were still ringing from the gunshots inside the tiny room. The metal of the gun was pressed against her cheek as she held her head in her hands. The acrid smell of burnt gunpowder emanated from the pistol.

She had shot two men. She had killed two human beings. She had ended their lives to save hers. She knew she'd never be the same again.

I'm a killer.

Does that make me no better than them?

CHAPTER 25

Grundy County, Illinois
Event + 4 days

Maddie lay curled into a ball, sobbing softly. She didn't know how much time had passed. She was jolted out of her crying fit by the shattering of glass. She sat up straight and pulled the gun close to her chest. Standing, she walked over to a clearing. A row of houses butted up to the woods. She couldn't tell which direction the breaking glass had come from. Crouching next to a tree, she listened, scanning each house for movement. After a moment, she saw a man emerge from a large yellow shed, two houses down from her position.

The man was carrying a barbeque grill like those used for tailgate parties. The man hadn't shut the door of the shed.

There may be something useful in there.

Probably not the food and water that she desperately needed right then, but maybe a tarp, rope, fishing line, or other things that might help her survive as she made her way to Uncle Ryan's house.

She thought for a moment. The men had only traveled a short distance from Darlene's farm before they stopped at the nasty trailer they'd held her in. If she could somehow make her way back to the trail, maybe she could find Darlene's farm.

She could find Emma.

Emma had probably run away when the two men had shown up. Maddie wanted to give Darlene and Ray Junior a proper burial, but she didn't think she could dig two graves. She'd try to cover them up, at least. They had been so good to her. She was afraid that she wouldn't encounter very many good people on the rest of her journey.

As she crept along the tree line to the shed, she looked to see if the man would return to shut the door. Maddie ran across the lawn and into the shed. She shoved the pistol into her pocket and rummaged through boxes and scanned the items on shelves. She bent over and flipped open the lid to a blue cooler under a small work bench and let out an audible sigh of relief when she discovered it was full of bottled water and energy drinks. Maddie unscrewed the top of one of the energy drinks and downed its contents.

Maddie looked around for something to carry the drinks in. Labeled storage totes lined the walls of the shed. Some totes were labeled "clothes." One said "books," and others said "photos" and "mementoes." The one that read "handbags and totes" caught Maddie's attention. Pleased that the owners were so well organized, Maddie opened the container and found a large L.L. Bean canvas tote bag. Opening a bottle of water, she took a sip and sat it down on a box. She wiped her mouth with the back of her hand and began filling the bag with as many bottles of water and drinks as would fit. After packing nine bottles, Maddie tried to zip the bag closed. It only zipped halfway, so she pulled one bottle out and held it under her chin as she finished zipping the tote closed. Gripping the bottle in one hand and the tote in another, she turned to go.

Maddie saw the man exiting a side door of the house. Dropping the bottle to the ground, she pulled the pistol from her pocket. She clutched it in her right hand, hoping she'd never have to use it again. Maddie ran across the yard. At the edge of the property where the lawn met the woods, Maddie stopped and crouched beside a tree to scan the area.

She tried to slow her breathing. The noise of her heart beating in her ears prevented her from hearing as sharply as she wanted. Closing her eyes, she inhaled, counted to three, then exhaled slowly. After a few seconds, her breathing had slowed. Maddie listened for any pursuers or dangers lurking in the woods.

Maddie inspected the pistol. Releasing the magazine, she counted the remaining rounds.

Only two rounds left. Shit.

She should have looked for the other guns before she left the trailer. But she had wanted the hell out of there before some other crazy druggies showed up.

Slapping the magazine back into the pistol, Maddie held it tight as she waited to see if the man had followed her. She wasn't sure if he had even seen her. Maybe she was being paranoid. She was drained, hungry, and filled with adrenaline from shooting two people.

She thought it was probably normal to be a little paranoid when running for her life in the apocalypse.

All she wanted in that moment was to get somewhere safe and sleep. Uncle Ryan's would be safe. She could sleep when she got there. Until then, she needed to keep moving.

After twenty minutes stumbling through the woods, Maddie came out on a trail beside the canal. Somehow, by some miracle, she had found her way back to the I&M Canal Trail. She looked around trying to get her bearings. The sun was high in the sky, so it was no help in giving her a direction at that moment. Taking a chance, she turned right and walked west. After ten minutes on the trail, she recognized a building. She had passed this before she got to the point near Darlene's farm.

She picked up her pace. She worked up to a run, but it was difficult with the oversized tote filled with heavy bottles. She slowed, holding the gun down at her side. She felt safer holding it. She picked up the pace again. Pumping her arms, she glanced at the pistol in her hand. She had run with full water flasks many times, but the weight of gun threw her off her pace.

Concentrate, Maddie. Remember your rhythmic breathing.

Left foot, inhale, right foot, left, right, exhale, repeat. Her pace quickened and her breathing slowed. She was in her groove.

It was only minutes before she came upon the spot where she had fallen near Darlene's driveway. She stopped at the junction of the trail and Darlene's gravel drive. She was full of dread and fear, but she had to check if Emma was all right—if Emma was still at the farmhouse.

She walked slowly down the driveway, pistol raised in front of her. She was startled by a rustling of leaves and sudden blur of motion to the side of her. As she turned, ready to fire, a large ball of white fur flung itself at her, putting his huge paws on her arms. She exhaled out loudly and lowered the gun. She had forgotten about the boy's dog, Cooper. Tears streamed down her face as she hugged the big dog to her chest. Ray Junior loved the dog. He had proudly told Maddie tales of the dog fighting off coyotes to protect his mother's goats. Cooper licked Maddie's face and wagged his tail.

Maddie stood, pulled up her baggy pants, and continued down the driveway. She stopped at the back corner of the house. The boy still lay where he had fallen.

What kind of coward shoots a kid in the back as he's running away?

He was no threat to them. Carl just killed him for sport. He was a sick man.

A sick, DEAD man, she thought, looking over at Ray Junior's body.

She no longer felt remorse for killing Kelly and Carl. She wasn't sure if her mom would understand, but she knew her dad would.

God would forgive her, she hoped.

Maddie ran up the back stairs and flung the door open. She dropped the canvas tote just inside the door and stiffened at the sight of Darlene's body. Darlene still lay on the floor in a huge pool of congealed blood. Placing the pistol on the counter, she called for Emma.

"Emma! Emma, it's me, Maddie. You can come out now. The bad men are gone," Maddie yelled, heading toward the front of the house.

Maddie searched room by room, calling Emma's name. When she reached the door to the basement, she heard a noise below. Maddie opened the door and called down.

"Emma, it's Maddie. You're safe now, please come out. We need to get out of here."

Emma emerged from around the corner with a shovel in her hands. She dropped the shovel and bounded up the stairs, flinging herself into Maddie's waiting arms.

The two hugged and cried for a moment before Maddie took Emma by the hand and led her out the front door. She sat Emma down on the front steps of the porch. Cooper stood beside her, his tail slapping Emma in the face.

"Wait here. I have to go in and find my pack. I need to fill the water bladder and get some food for the road."

"No, don't leave me, Maddie."

"I'll just be a minute, I promise. Cooper here will keep you company. Won't you, big guy," Maddie said, ruffling the dog's fur.

Maddie returned to the kitchen. Stepping over Darlene, Maddie retrieved the tote bag full of bottled water and returned to the front porch. Placing the bag next to Emma, Maddie returned to the kitchen. Ray Junior's body was visible from the kitchen window.

Getting Ray Junior's body up the stairs and into the house was difficult. Maddie could tell she had used all her physical reserves. She was running on empty. She knew all too well what happened when you pushed your body to the extreme without providing it proper nutrition. She'd have to eat soon, but first she needed to pay respect to Darlene and her son.

Maddie retrieved a quilt from Darlene's bed. Placing Ray Junior next to his mother, she covered the two bodies with the quilt. Maddie looked down at them. She thanked them for their kindness. She placed a bouquet of flowers she had plucked from Darlene's garden on top of the quilt.

A lump formed in Maddie's throat. Tears threatened to cloud her vision again. She fought back the tears.

Maddie didn't have time for grief. She was still at least twenty miles from Uncle Ryan's house. She and Emma needed to fuel up their bodies and get back on the trail. If they pushed, they could be there by dark. Uncle Ryan may even have hot water for a bath if his solar panels still worked. She dreamed of taking a nice, long, hot bath.

Maddie opened the door to the pantry. She unscrewed the lid on a jar of peanut butter and scooped some out with her fingers, transferring it to her mouth. She took a plastic shopping bag from the pantry as she chewed. She put the jar of peanut butter and a package of crackers in the bag, then grabbed two cans of soup and a can of mixed fruit. She found a spoon in a drawer and pulling the tab to open one of them, then proceeded to eat it cold, straight out of the can.

After rummaging around in all the cabinet drawers, Maddie found a can opener. She opened the can of fruit and a can of chicken noodle soup, grabbed another spoon, and headed for the porch.

"I know the soup is cold, but you need to eat as much of it as you can. We need to eat to fuel our bodies so we can make it to my uncle's house today," Maddie said, setting the bag down and handing Emma the two cans and the spoon.

Before Emma could get the first spoonful of soup into her mouth, Cooper stuck his nose into the can and knocked it to the ground.

"It's okay. He must be hungry," Emma said, petting the dog.

Returning to the pantry, Maddie found a bag of dog food and filled the largest bowl she could find. When she pushed open the screen door, Cooper rushed over to her. Maddie placed the bowl down on the step in front of the dog. He licked the bowl clean and begged for more. She pulled a bottle of water from the tote and poured it into the bowl. He lapped it dry in seconds.

Maddie knew a person could go thirty days without food, but likely only a couple of days without water. They would need to hydrate themselves, especially if they had to run for their lives.

Returning to the kitchen, Maddie opened another can of soup and took it to Emma. Emma sat on the porch and ate. Maddie remembered the food in the smoker and the dehydrating vegetables. With no one to tend the fire, the meat in the smoker would be bad, but the vegetables were still good. Maddie used a second plastic bag to gather the dehydrated veggies.

Maddie retrieved her runner's vest pack from the bedroom. The knife and hatchet were still attached to the pack. She removed her sleeping bag and rain jacket to make room for the food. She stuffed the dehydrated veggies and jar of peanut butter inside. After filling the water bladder and soft flasks, Maddie slid her arms into the vest and pulled the V straps tight across her chest.

She retrieved the pistol from the counter in the kitchen, even though it only had two rounds left. Hopefully, two rounds would be all she needed if it came to it. Both Darlene and Ray Junior's shotguns were missing. A search of the house revealed that the Goff brothers had taken all their weapons and ammo.

Returning to the porch, Maddie took two bottles of water from the canvas tote and refilled the dog's water bowl. The rest she left sitting on the steps. They were too heavy and awkward to carry.

Standing on Darlene's front porch, Maddie looked toward the trail. It didn't seem right to leave Darlene and Ray Junior in the house like that, but she thought maybe she and Uncle Ryan might return and give them a proper burial.

Maddie and Emma descended the steps. Turning toward the house, Maddie said a silent thank you to Darlene and Ray Junior. The two headed off toward the I&M Canal Trail. Cooper followed them. Maddie stopped and looked down at the dog. He stopped and sat on her foot. She reached down and patted Cooper on the head.

"I'll see you, boy."

Maddie and Emma turned and walked toward the trail. The dog sprang up behind them and ran off down the driveway. When Maddie and Emma reached him, he turned and walked beside Emma. Emma looked questioningly up at Maddie. Maddie nodded, and the trio picked up the pace to a jog. Ray Junior would be happy his beloved dog would have a new home. She was sure of it.

When they reached the town of Seneca, Illinois, Maddie slowed and held her arm out to stop Emma. Cooper ran over and sat at Emma's feet. Maddie pulled the map from her pack and searched for an alternative route. She was not comfortable traveling through a town.

Finding there wasn't another route that didn't require crossing water, Maddie and Emma walked into town. Stopping just before crossing the first city street, Maddie placed the pistol she had been carrying in the kangaroo pouch of her pack. People might not appreciate her running through their town with a pistol in her hand.

Surprisingly, the town looked untouched by the violence that they had seen in other cities on their trip.

Not wanting to push their luck, Maddie picked up the pace. Emma reached down and took a hold of Cooper's collar. There were a few people on the streets, but not many. No one was near the trail. Maddie was grateful for that.

After passing the last city street in Seneca, Maddie and Emma breathed a sigh of relief. They picked up the pace and started jogging away from town. When they came to a section of the trail that was not very well maintained, they were forced to slow. Grass grew on the path and tall weeds lined the trail on both sides, slapping at their arms as they ran. At one point, there were tree limbs down over the road. It took a great deal of extra energy to climb over them.

When Maddie saw a sign for Marseilles, her heart leapt. She was close. She recalled that Uncle Ryan lived just outside of town. They continued on the trail until it crossed over Main Street. When they reached Main Street, they turned right and walked south, crossing over the Illinois River. Maddie and Emma jogged as they left town and saw open fields. At a junction, they continued straight. At the end of the road sat an old yellow farmhouse. She stopped and stared at the house. She looked over to Emma and down at Cooper, who sat at her side.

"We're here. We made it. We'll be safe now, don't you worry. Uncle Ryan is really nice, and he loves dogs," Maddie said, ruffling the fur on his head.

She brushed the fur from his eyes, and the three of them took off running as fast as they could. When she reached the mailbox, Maddie stopped. She stared at the house. It was the typical Midwest farmhouse, surrounded by plowed fields and a large red barn in the back. A long gravel drive divided two fields where cows and horses grazed peacefully. Maddie smiled and pointed at a foal running around its mother. Emma smiled broadly.

Lazy black calves dotted the pasture.

Movement at the barn caught Maddie's attention. Maddie halted, suddenly worried that it wasn't Uncle Ryan. She saw the man raise his weapon. No doubt they were in the man's rifle scope. She pushed Emma behind her.

What if she had come to the wrong house? It had been years since she had been there. What if he had moved and not told her? What if something had happened to him and bad men had taken over the place?

Maddie wanted to turn and run. She was just about to do exactly that before Cooper took off at a full run toward the man. Maddie and Emma ran after him, calling his name and demanding that he stop, but he kept going.

When he reached the man, Cooper leapt up and put his paws on the man's chest and licked his face. When Uncle Ryan looked around the side of the large mass of fur, Maddie took off at full sprint with Emma right behind her. Maddie flung herself into him and melted into his embrace. Ryan's arms wrapped around her, enveloping her like a cocoon. Maddie felt the release of all the fear and pain. She hung there in Ryan's arms, sobbing uncontrollably. Ryan held her and stroked her hair just like her dad use too. She knew that she was finally safe.

Just like her dad, Ryan would do whatever he had to make sure of that. They had made it. She'd made it. She was no longer alone in the apocalypse.

CHAPTER 26

Joint Field Offices
  Marseilles, Illinois
  Event + 4 days

The last time Aims had seen everyone together in the same room had been during their last emergency operations exercise. This time, however, there were a lot more empty chairs. Everyone in the Joint Field Office coordination meeting wore somber faces. Most looked as if they hadn't slept since the event. Everyone except Principal Federal Officer, Sarah Wilms. Wilms wore a crisp pressed business suit and black flats. Her hair was in a tight bun. From what Aims could recall of the woman, she always looked serious. If she were concerned about the state of the country in the current crisis, she didn't show it.

No doubt Wilms would have liked to wait until the governor's representative had arrived, but with such important matters to address, waiting was a courtesy of their old world.

"I'm sorry to have held up the meeting," Wilms said. "I was just made aware of a critical issue at Clint Power Station. One of their emergency generators is inoperable, and one other is low on diesel due to a fuel leak. Out of an abundance of caution, I've ordered the Red Cross shelter in Decatur closed. The refugees at that shelter will be distributed among existing shelters in other parts of the state."

She paused and looked around the room.

"DHS has requested that some refugees from the Decatur facility be brought here to JCO until they can be interviewed and cleared for release back into their communities. I've granted that request."

"What about the other five nuclear power plants? Specifically, the four near here?" the emergency manager for Bloomington asked.

"I've been assured that operations are being shut down at this time. When their generators begin to run low on diesel, they'll switch the cooling tower pumps to solar power. They're testing that system now. I should receive a report from them by tomorrow. We'll continue to monitor the situation. They have assured me that there isn't any threat of meltdown. Everyone will be provided with potassium iodide tablets, but we do not anticipate any issues with the reactors."

Wilms's assistant hung a chart on an easel before taking a seat next to her.

After an hour of discussing duties and logistics, Wilms dismissed the group. Aims was the first to head to the door. He'd spent the better part of his career in governmental meetings. It was one of the few things they did well. They even conducted meetings to discuss how to have a meeting.

Aims headed straight for the Department of Homeland Security tent. The DHS team was huddled over a map spread out on a long table. Areas were circled in different colors. As a regional operating center, they were responsible for six states. Aims only saw two other state officials present.

He was shocked to see General Walter Dempsey seated beside

his deputy director, Samone Perez. He had been told Dempsey was in D.C. at the time of the event. Perez was the only member of the group to acknowledge Aims. The others barely raised their eyes from the map.

"We have secured all the major commercial ports except for the Port of Detroit. The railyards have been a challenge due to their proximity to heavily populated areas. They remain a priority mission. Transit is working to get trucks there to offload supplies as fast as possible and minimize loss," the DHS official said.

After the status briefing, Aims cornered Perez before she could leave.

"What's up?" he asked, pointing to the general.

At first, she tried to dodge his question, but he grabbed her by the arm and moved her away from the exiting group.

"Tell me, Perez. I know you know something."

Perez looked over her shoulder before answering.

"He received an intelligence report prior to his scheduled flight. That is all I can tell you, Aims."

"Oh hell, Perez, stop being cryptic. You know you're going to tell me, either here and now or in bed tonight. So, spill it."

Perez glared at Aims.

As her superior, he should have been the one with all the answers. But to his chagrin, she was the one having an affair with a top intelligence official. She had gladly shared her secrets before the event. Her unwillingness now led him to believe that she either didn't know much or she was using it for leverage with the folks at the top of the new government.

She hesitated.

He squeezed her arm tighter.

"Not here. I'll tell you everything I know tonight."

She gave him a coy smile before jerking her arm away. He watched her walk out of the tent before he approached the DHS field officer. Being in charge of logistics, he needed to coordinate the use of vehicles and personnel. With over half of their fleet of stockpiled buses inoperable, they had been forced to pull assets from the relief effort to transport personnel to secure critical infrastructure. That did not sit well with the local jurisdictions.

"What is this about us housing refugees from the shelters that are closing?" Aims asked the field officer.

"Those guys down there in Decatur think we have time to conduct background checks on disgruntled citizens. For the life of me, I don't know why Wilms allowed it. We have enough on our hands without babysitting rowdy citizens."

"I agree. That is why I am not buying it. Wilms is too sharp to allow resources to be wasted that way. You said they had been designated troublemakers. Were they designated troublemakers before or after the event?" Aims asked.

The field officer shrugged before picking up his belongings and exiting the tent. Aims stared down at the map. Illinois, Indiana, Wisconsin, Minnesota, Michigan, and Ohio were depicted. Some cities were circled in black with Xs marked through them, including Chicago, Detroit, and Milwaukee. Indianapolis stood out as it was the only city on the entire map with a green circle. Aims took that to mean only one large metropolitan area had been secured four days after the event.

How long before we lose control of that city as well?

CHAPTER 27

Red Cross Disaster Shelter
  Decatur Airport
  Decatur, Illinois,
  Event + 4 days

The lawnmower-like clatter of electric generators had drowned out most of the snoring and coughing in the troublemaker tent. A Red Cross volunteer came to lead the group to a large white tent where breakfast was being served. Zach sat with James and his son. Although the eggs were rubbery, the gravy was good and served to smother the bland taste, providing a semi-satisfying and filling breakfast. Bottles of hot sauce were provided and smothered lingering blandness as well. After all those peanut butter sandwiches at the church, the hot meal was nice.

After breakfast, the group had been allowed to spend the rest of the morning in a tent set up with tables, folding chairs, books, and board games. Zach hadn't seen the guards since the night before. When they had been moved from tent to tent, he couldn't see the rest of the camp or even where within the camp they were.

"You want to play a game of Sorry with us?" James's son asked.

"Sure," Zach said, taking a seat across from James.

Zach wasn't interested in playing board games. He needed information. He had a decision to make. He needed to know as much as possible about where they were so he could form a plan to get home.

Zach leaned in.

"James, did you hear the two men in the corner over there talking about being taken to a different shelter today?"

"Yeah, that Asian guy said he had been in the porta-john when he overheard some workers coordinating plans to take a group of us to another camp to meet up with the buses heading south."

"You believe them? About meeting up with buses heading south, I mean?" Zach whispered.

"It makes sense that they would coordinate routes that way. Even the Greyhound buses have hubs where you go to be routed in different directions."

"I guess. It's just... I heard that FEMA had camps all over. It also makes sense that they would move all the troublemakers like us to a different camp. Maybe one a little more secure."

"Where did you hear that?" asked James.

"YouTube."

"I think you've listened to too many conspiracy theories."

"Some of them seemed plausible."

"You do know that a lot of that stuff has been debunked, right?" James said with a condescending expression.

"Yeah, I know some of it has, but there's a little truth in every-thing, right?"

"I don't see where we have a lot of choice but to comply and go where they tell us at this point. You see what resisting got us."

"That is what I don't like about all this. How come they have the right to detain us like this? They take our stuff and won't let us leave. That is not American. We haven't had any due process. What about illegal search and seizure?" Zach asked.

"It is all different when there's a national emergency declared. Our nation has been attacked, and I am sure they are working to sort it all out. I am grateful to be here rather than out there on the interstate without food and water. Before we came here, we saw people being robbed at the exit where we were."

"If I had left when all this happened, I'd be home by now. I bet I still could get myself home faster than these people can if they would just give me my pack back." Zach leaned back in his chair and crossed his arms across his chest.

James chuffed through his nose.

"I was once full of piss and vinegar like you, so I understand you think that's the case, but it's not the same world it was a week ago. I imagine by now, it's even less so. You're better off just being patient and allowing them time to get everything worked out. They'll get us all home, eventually. Though, I am not sure what home will look like now. Six days without electricity, all the food in my fridge and freezer will be spoiled. I'm not sure I'll even have running water at my house."

"It'll probably be dangerous in the cities. With no food delivery to the stores, people will be looting houses by now," Zach said.

James looked to his son.

"Oh. I hadn't thought of that. We had trouble with people breaking into houses before all this. Now that I think about it, I'm not sure I'd want to return home. Sounds like my boy and me are better off right here until this mess is over."

Neither of them spoke for several minutes. James's son set up the board game and smiled, eager to play. Zach went through the motions of playing the game, but he was distracted by thoughts of his own home. Being a suburb of St. Louis, Missouri, it had likely already become a fight to survive the theft and looting there. With the EMP hitting during the workday, most of Clarkson Valley's residents would have been at work, leaving many houses empty.

Zach thought of his stepdad, Jason. He had stayed home while his mother and sister had traveled to California to care for Zach's grandmother.

Jason's dental practice was located in the neighboring town of Chesterfield. He had probably walked home, but he was ill-equipped to defend their house from invading criminals. Unlike Greg, Jason didn't like guns and didn't know how to use them. His mother had insisted on keeping theirs when they moved in with Jason after the wedding, but he made them keep them in a gun safe in the basement. Zach wasn't sure he even knew the combination. The safe was a top-of-the-line model, bolted to the concrete floor, so there was a high probability that the guns would still be there when he got home. What food stores and preps they had brought with them from their old house would likely have been taken by now.

"Where did you say your parents were?" James asked, breaking the silence.

"My mom is at my Grand and Grandpa Frank's house in San Diego. My sister was in the airport in Chicago when this hit."

"Oh, man. You must be worried for her."

"I am. But I'm not as worried for my mom. she's lots of prepared people we know out there. But my sister is alone in that huge city. I just hope she remembers what our dad taught us and has left the city already."

"That'd be dangerous for a girl alone. She'd probably be safer staying in the airport until the Red Cross or someone comes for them."

"If she is smart, she got out of there before it got crazy. I am hoping she remembered the way to my dad's friend's farm just west of Chicago. He can keep her safe and get her home."

"I bet she did just that. She's probably sitting at home right now. You have to think positive. I bet the Red Cross and FEMA are working on getting your mom home soon too."

"Could be."

After all he had learned about the government's ability to 'help' in disaster situations, Zach doubted it. Their responses to past hurricanes and flooding had made that clear. Zach knew it was likely that the whole nation had been crippled by the EMP. Emergency services and disaster relief agencies would be overwhelmed and running on reduced staff due to lack of transportation and communications.

Most of the country would be on their own, likely for a very long time.

The three of them passed the time playing board games and cards. After lunch, the group lined up to return to the recreation tent. A man and a woman with clipboards stood at the entrance. After they asked his name, Zach was led to another tent at the end of a long row of tents. He could see several buses parked nearby. He was directed to stand in another long line. He watched as people proceeded through the line, one-by-one, then onto a bus. When Zach reached the head of the line, a man with a clipboard asked for his name. The man flipped through pages and checked it off, then handed Zach a card with a bus number written on it.

"I came here with my high school class. Can you look and see if they have left already?" Zach asked.

The man flipped through his pages again.

"They left yesterday," he said, motioning for the next in line to move forward.

Zach was led to the second of three buses. Before getting on, Zach asked, "What about my backpack? Am I going to get that back?"

"All personal belongings have already been loaded," said another man with a clipboard.

"My inventory shows that you had one bag, and it has been loaded on this bus."

The man on the other side of him motioned for Zach to board the bus. As he boarded the bus and walked down the aisle to find a seat, he passed the Marine from the church. They both gave a slight nod of mutual acknowledgment as Zach proceeded to the back of the bus and took a seat.

All the buses pulled up to a double gate. Zach watched as two turned left and then his bus turned right and headed north to Interstate 55.

The bus rolled through a few small towns. Zach tried to memorize the names in case he got a chance to get off and away from the bus. As the bus drove past Pontiac, it exited the interstate onto a county road. As they drove through the town of Ransom, a crowd from a convenience store stepped into the road, causing the driver to swerve.

Zach and his fellow passengers were tossed around in their seats. Some fell to the floor. Zach stood and reached down to help a middle-aged woman get back to her seat. Zach looked up just in time to see a large box truck racing toward them. He dropped back into his seat and braced himself for impact. As they reached the middle of the intersection, the truck T-boned them. The bus rolled onto its side and skidded to a stop against a concrete lane barrier.

Zach was pinned between the window and a large man. With all his strength, he managed to pull himself out from under the man. Injured passengers lay in heaps on top of the windows. Bodies were wrapped around seatbacks. He could tell they were badly injured with broken bones and head wounds. He reached down and pulled the handle on the back door. Jumping to the ground, he helped pull a mother and child out of the bus, followed by a middle-aged man.

He counted six walking wounded in total. The majority of the passengers were severely injured and unable to get out of the bus by themselves. Zach ran over to the box truck. It lay on its side in a parking lot, smoke billowing from its crushed front end. The driver lay unconscious or dead in the street. Zach ran over to the man, kneeling to check for a pulse. He hesitated. There was so much blood. The driver's eyes were open. He was bleeding from mouth, nose, eyes, and ears. Zach reached down and placed two fingers on the man's neck. He didn't detect a pulse. He pulled his hand back and stood. He stared at the blood on his fingers then wiped it on his jeans.

People ran out of nearby houses and businesses. Zach helped a mother wrap a torn T-shirt around her son's injured arm and leg.

"My other son is still on the bus. Can you stay with him while I go?" she asked.

"Go, go, I've got this. Yell if you need help," Zach called after her.

It was quieter than Zach thought it should be. At first, there was screaming and yelling in the immediate aftermath. But now there were only low moans coming from the bus. After what seemed to be an eternity, a police officer and some type of medical personnel arrived. When the mother didn't return, Zach asked a woman nearby to sit with the young boy. He found the mother rocking an older boy in her arms. He didn't appear to be alive.

Zach helped remove passengers from the bus and laid them in a parking lot where a makeshift triage had been set up. The deceased were left on the bus, including the bus driver and his partner, the only Red Cross officials onboard.

Zach walked up and down the two short rows of survivors. There were so few. He expected there to be more. Maybe if there had been a functioning hospital, more would have survived. Just a week ago, an ambulance would have transported the injured to a local emergency room. They would have been triaged and those requiring lifesaving treatment would have been flown to a trauma center. The ones who received treatment before the golden hour was over may have lived.

As he walked by looking for the boy he had helped, an arm reached out and grabbed hold of his pants leg.

"You should do it now."

Stopping suddenly, Zach looked down. It was the Marine from the church. His head was bandaged as well as his arm and both legs.

"I'm sorry, what did you say?" Zach asked.

The man motioned for Zach to lean down. Zach took a knee beside the man.

"You need to see if you can get your pack and get out of here before they send reinforcements," the man said in a low voice.

Zach hadn't thought about taking the opportunity to escape. His gaze went from the man to the bus.

"There's nothing you can do for anyone here. You go and find your family."

"I'm not really sure where we are. Without a map, I might end up in Kansas or Indiana before I realized I went the wrong way."

"You need to get to the interstate. It runs north to south. You can figure out directions, can't you?"

"Yeah."

"We just went past Pontiac. If you go back the way we came on this road, you will run right into Interstate 55. Where is home?"

"Missouri. St. Louis, Missouri."

"Take this road to the interstate and follow it south. It runs right into St. Louis."

"How far are we from Chicago, do you think?"

"About a hundred miles or so. You don't want to go there. That is the opposite direction from St. Louis," the man said, resting his hand on his bandaged head to shield his eyes from the sun.

"I know. It's just —" He paused. "It is just that my sister was in the airport in Chicago when the lights went out."

"Listen to me, kid. You don't want to go anywhere near the city. It'll be total chaos by now. Your sister probably got picked up by FEMA like we did. In that case, you won't find her in Chicago. They will have locked that city down by now just to contain the situation."

"Where would FEMA have taken her?"

"My guess is Marseilles. They have a joint FEMA/National Guard training facility there. That is where this bus was headed."

"I read about that place," Zach said. "My dad's—"

He started to say that his dad's friend lived near there, but he stopped himself. He didn't want to divulge any information that FEMA could use to find him.

He'd go to Ryan's and the two of them would go to that FEMA camp and get his sister. He just hoped that she was there. Like the man had said, going into Chicago would be a bad decision.

CHAPTER 28

Masters' Farm
Marseilles, Illinois
Event +5 days

The pre-dawn crowing of Foghorn, the rooster, was something Maddie didn't think she'd ever get accustomed to, nor did she want to. Although she woke early to run before school, being awakened before daylight was still not something she enjoyed.

Ryan was already up. She could tell by the smell of fresh-brewed coffee wafting in from the kitchen.

Thank God for coffee.

Conditioned through his years in the military, Ryan had always been an early riser.

Looking over to a still-sleeping Emma, Maddie contemplated getting out of bed. She picked up a lock of Emma's curly red hair and spun it around her fingers. She'd always wanted a little sister. This just wasn't how she imagined she'd get one.

Ryan had offered Emma her own room, but after the ordeal of the last few days, she requested to stay with Maddie.

Maddie pulled the quilt over Emma's exposed arm and ran a hand over the plaid fabric that had once been Ryan's dad's shirt. She had helped Ryan's mother stitch the quilt on her last visit there.

Sliding out from under the covers, Maddie placed her feet on the floor, stretched, and pulled on Mamaw Masters's bathrobe. Ryan's mother had passed several years earlier, but he had yet to pack away her things. At that moment, Maddie missed her greatly. She had been as close with Mamaw Masters as she had with her biological grandmother.

She pulled up the collar and inhaled. It smelled freshly washed. Mamaw Masters made her own soap, shampoo, and household cleaners from materials she grew on the farm, so everything in the home had its own pleasant herbal aroma. She sold her soaps along with fresh herbs, flowers, and eggs at a local farmers' market.

Leaving the door open a crack so she could hear Emma, Maddie made her way down the long hall. A well-worn path in the hardwood floor led the way to the kitchen at the back of the farmhouse.

"Did Foghorn wake you?" Ryan chuckled.

"He did," Maddie said, yawning.

After pouring herself a cup of coffee, Maddie pulled a stool away from the island and took a seat across from Ryan.

"Tell me again, why on earth do you have a mean rooster who crows before daylight?" she asked, rubbing sleep from her eyes.

"You don't need me to explain the birds and the bees to you— or do you?" Ryan chuckled.

After taking a long drink of his coffee, he gently set the mug back on the counter. He ran his hand down the length of his long, sandy brown beard. It was at least six inches longer than the last time Maddie had seen it. The beard grew in contradiction with his close-cropped hair.

Catching movement from the corner of her eye, she spotted Emma in the doorway. She hugged the door frame and peeked her head into the kitchen.

Maddie walked over and gave her a hug.

Ruffling Emma's wild, untamed hair, she asked, "How did you sleep, Em?"

"Okay," Emma said. With her arms around Maddie's waist, she looked past her to where Ryan sat.

Maddie leaned down and whispered in her ear, "It's okay. He's family."

"You want some breakfast? I got bacon and eggs," Ryan said, getting to his feet.

If Maddie hadn't seen it for herself, she wouldn't have believed the world had gone to shit. Nothing at the farm was different. The lights were on. The stove worked. She had hot coffee and was about to have eggs and bacon for breakfast.

Maddie took Emma's hand and helped her onto a barstool next to her. Ryan set plates of bacon, eggs, and toast before them. Maddie almost cried, it looked so good.

"You don't really appreciate good food until you think you'll never taste it again," Maddie said, snapping a crisp piece of bacon in two.

Ryan stared at Emma as she greedily forked fluffy scrambled eggs into her mouth. She looked up, and he smiled back at her.

"These are amazing," Emma said. Her green eyes sparkled.

"Thanks," he said.

"You know, you remind me of someone. Are you famous?" Ryan asked.

Emma looked to Maddie before shaking her head.

"You sure? I could have sworn I saw you in a commercial for a movie."

He snapped his fingers and pointed to Emma.

"I know who you are. You played the girl in Brave," Ryan joked.

"Don't say it," Maddie warned.

Emma lowered her chin and gave Ryan the stink-eye.

Maddie leaned in close to Ryan and whispered, "She hates that movie. The boys used to tease her. Whatever you do, don't call her Merida."

"You're Merida," Ryan bellowed.

Maddie turned to Emma.

"Let's get him," Emma said as she scooped egg onto her fork and flicked it at Ryan.

Emma squealed as Ryan opened his mouth and attempted to catch the scrambled eggs the girls were hurling at him.

"Okay! Okay! I'm sorry. It won't happen again. The next person who throws food has to do all the dishes," he laughed, shielding his face with his arm.

The girls dropped their forks on their plates. Maddie pointed to Ryan's beard, and the two broke out in uncontrollable giggles.

Ryan stood and brushed egg from his shirt and shook his beard over the sink.

"There are four more pieces of bacon over here. If you two can stop cackling, I might let you have them."

"I love bacon. I didn't think I'd ever taste it again. This here is heaven," Maddie said, stuffing more into her already full mouth.

Staring at her plate, Maddie thought a meal like this demonstrated the difference between being prepared or unprepared for the apocalypse. Ryan had been prepared. Her dad had been somewhat responsible for that fact. He had pestered Ryan for two years before Ryan gave in and went to conventions and meetups with him to learn the skills required to pull all this off. It had brought them all even closer as a family.

Ryan had come down every summer and drilled with them at the cabin in Texas County. He had brought his buddies down once. They had practiced perimeter security, and her dad had shown them how to survive in the woods. Those had been Maddie's least favorite drills. She hated the primitive camping. She drew the line at eating bugs, but Zach loved to gross her out by eating grasshoppers.

"I've got two freezers full of meat and vegetables. That, along with the chickens, pigs, goats, cows, and horses, makes me totally self-sufficient here on this little slice of paradise."

An old wood cook stove still sat in the corner opposite its more modern counterpart. The same rooster-print curtains hung above the window over the sink. A wooden dough box and a cheese vat table lined one wall. Cabinets were sparse. The kitchen looked like it had one foot in the nineteenth century and the other in the twenty-first.

"After we finish up here, I'll show you my setup. You'll probably recognize some of it. I used a lot of your dad's designs."

"He'd be proud that they've helped you," Maddie said.

"Tomorrow, we can run over to see a buddy of mine. He's a ham operator. We can see if his radios still work. If they do, maybe we can get some idea how it is in California."

"Can we? That'd be awesome. I've tried not to worry about Mom. I know she wouldn't leave Grand and Grandpa to fend for themselves, so she'd stay put. I worry about things getting rough there in San Diego."

"Your mom is very smart and resourceful. For all her bluster about your dad's preps and drills, she paid attention and knows her stuff. She knows where to go out there to get any resources she needs. Your dad had contacts there. If she needs help, she knows what to do."

He sipped his black coffee. He still drank from the same Marine Corps mug she remembered. The image of that mug was seared in her mind. The last time she had stayed there, she had made the mistake of washing it—with soap. Ryan hadn't been happy about that. Mamaw Masters said he thought washing it would ruin the flavor of the coffee. He hadn't washed it since he came home from Afghanistan. He'd drink coffee from it all day, then before bed, he'd rinse it out and put it on the windowsill in the kitchen.

Maddie pointed to the mug.

"You want me to wash that for you?" she laughed, standing and picking up her plate.

Ryan balled his hands into fists and shook them at her.

"You keep your paws off my mug this time, missy, or else we're going toe-to-toe."

Returning to her seat at the island, she placed her elbows on the counter. Laying her head in her hands, she stared out the window. Dawn had arrived without fanfare.

"You think Zach and Mom are okay? You think they will make it home?"

"I know they will. Don't worry, Maddie. They know how to survive just like you do."

"But it is rough out there, Uncle Ryan. It is worse than I could've ever imagined, and it has only been a couple of days. Hell, people were looting and killing people within hours in Chicago."

Ryan scratched his head. He looked down at his nearly empty mug.

"People did that before the power went out. That is nothing new for the Windy City."

"They lit the police station on fire," Maddie said.

"I imagine that'd be the first thing some of them would do. They didn't have respect for law enforcement before, and now they have their chance to really show their frustrations."

Maddie straightened and stretched. She was still sore from her fall on the trail and the rough handling by the brothers. She studied the new bandages Ryan had put on her wrists and ankles after they arrived. She thought about how good it had felt to crawl into a real bed with crisp, clean sheets. She yawned and arched her back.

"Don't even think about going back to bed. We have work to do. Those eggs don't collect themselves. I already milked the goats, but they'll need fresh hay and water. And that dog of yours will need a doghouse," he said, pointing back and forth between Maddie and Emma.

Maddie chuffed.

"He isn't our dog. Me and Emma are his humans. He chose us."

Emma grinned and nodded.

"How many chickens do you have?" Maddie said.

"Oh, about thirty, I'd say. There are a few ducks and turkeys mixed in with them too that I picked up at auctions." He paused. "Speaking of chickens, we should take eggs with us to give Earl. I'm sure his wife is ready for something not from a can or MRE by now."

"Earl is the ham operator? You think he could find someone to get a message to Mom?" Maddie asked.

Ryan paused and took another sip of coffee. He got up and poured himself another cup.

"Fill up?" he said, pointing to Maddie's mug.

She nodded, and Ryan filled her cup. Placing the pot back on the stove, Ryan turned and stared out the window over the sink.

Growing impatient for an answer, Maddie asked, "Do you think he knows anyone in San Diego?"

"I don't know about specifically San Diego, but I know he has contacts out in California."

"Why didn't you ever get a ham radio? I know my dad talked about getting into it, but…"

"I didn't make it a priority. I figured since I knew a few in the area, I'd focus on other things. You have to do what you can with the resources you have, and I put security above communications —at least that type of comms." Ryan returned to his seat across from Maddie.

"It looks like you've done a good job preparing, from what I can see. It was amazing coming here and having a hot shower and cold drinks."

"We have your dad to thank for that," Ryan said, looking toward the ceiling.

Maddie gave a slight nod.

An awkward silence fell between them.

Maddie rose and walked over to the sink. As she washed her coffee mug, she looked out past the rose garden to the pasture dotted with cows, goats, and horses. The chickens pecked and scratched around the barn. Cooper slowly rose from the hole he had dug in the loose dirt in front of the barn doors and walked over to the porch steps. Craning her neck, she watched the big white dog plop down and stretch out. He looked like he was settling in just fine. She supposed he missed Ray Junior and Darlene. The memory of their lifeless bodies lying on the floor of their kitchen brought a wave of nausea. Her heart pounded in her ears. She could barely hear what Ryan was saying.

"Before you or Emma go outside, I need to show you both the perimeter defenses I've set up around the property. Most are out along the property line, so you won't have to worry much about them at the moment. There are a few motion sensors near the barn, garden, and chicken coops. There are a few more low-tech alerts in places that might startle you. You should know about those before you go wandering around. They aren't dangerous or anything, but they'll scare the crap outta you if you set one off."

"How do you keep the animals from tripping them?" Maddie asked, returning to her seat.

"Right now, they are set at chest height."

Emma leaned over and whispered in Maddie's ear. Maddie pointed to the powder room just off the kitchen.

After Emma shut the door, Ryan said, "Emma might not be as strong as you are, Maddie. She'll need our help to process all that happened."

Looking up, he continued, "That's part of the reason I wanted to show you both my security systems. When I got back, I had a hard time feeling safe anywhere. Helping your dad with the perimeter defense plan at the hunting cabin showed me I could take control of things in my life. It helped me to be able to make a safe space for myself. When I was in Afghanistan, I had my team, and we had the ability to defend ourselves as well as be on the offense. When we were back at base, we had walls and razor wire and guards at the gates. Back here at home, I felt exposed."

Maddie nodded. "I know what that feels like. That is why I felt so much relief when we got here. I felt safe for the first time since this whole mess started."

"I want you and Emma to help me with the last of my perimeter defense plans for that reason too. Being a part of a team and taking back control of your own safety can really boost your sense of security. But we can't get too comfortable. Soon, the cities will run out of resources and the scavengers will come."

Maddie raised her eyebrows. She knew what he was saying was true. She had seen it already in the city. She'd done it herself. She wanted to pretend a little longer that the chaos wouldn't come near them there on the farm.

"I have people coming soon. Friends. A group like your dad had set up of like-minded people willing to pull together and make it through this," Ryan said.

He looked for a response.

Maddie was quiet, lost in thought. She remembered the group her dad had gathered. She'd trained with them at the hunting cabin. She'd seen very little of them after her dad died, though, especially after her mother had married Jason. Jason thought the whole prepper thing was crazy, paranoid redneck stuff. He had said so— out loud—to her dad's friends.

"When are they getting here?" Maddie asked, returning her gaze to Ryan.

"I imagine they are all heading this way now. Most live here in Illinois. They are single men, without families. We kinda thought we'd stick together, maybe join a larger group after everything settled down."

"Do I know any of them?" Maddie asked.

"You know Rank and Lugnut. The others are guys from the

local gun club. They are veterans too, mostly Army, but we don't hold that against them," Ryan said, grinning.

Maddie beamed. Lugnut was one of her favorites from her dad's group. He was never serious about anything, but he was seriously scary if you pissed him off. She was particularly happy she'd be seeing Rank again. She felt better already knowing those guys would join them.

"I'm looking forward to seeing them again. Are they all sporting Duck Dynasty beards too?" she asked, reaching over and flicking the end of his beard. He swatted her hand away.

"Don't fear the beard," he said, chuckling before continuing, "I know they will be happy to see you here safe and sound." Ryan trailed off, staring into his coffee mug.

Maddie stared at it too as if it possessed some power that might reveal the whereabouts of her mother and brother. That question nearly consumed her. The not-knowing was agonizing. She couldn't imagine what parents of missing children must endure. She hoped that Ryan's ham operator friend could tell them something about how things were in California. Maybe even in San Diego itself. Any news was better than nothing. Her imagination ran wild in the void of information.

A low growl at the back steps roused Maddie from her thoughts. Looking through the screen door, she watched Cooper. He stood with his hackles raised and his tail held high. He sniffed the air then took off. His barking trailed off toward the front of the house.

Ryan stood, grabbed a rifle leaning in the corner, and ran toward the front door.

"Maddie, get Emma. Stay in the bedroom until you hear from me," Ryan called over his shoulder.

The bathroom door flew open and Emma peered out, her eyes wide with fear. Maddie shot to her feet, grabbed Emma's arm, and the two ran down the hall.

"Maddie, what is going on?" Emma asked.

Ignoring the girl's questions, Maddie went straight to her pack. After retrieving the pistol she had taken from her kidnappers, she rushed over to the bed. Grabbing Emma by the hand, she pulled her gently to the floor.

"Stay down, Emma."

"What is going on?" Emma whined.

"I'm not sure. It could be nothing. Cooper is barking and went running down the driveway. It could be just a cat or something. Uncle Ryan went to check it out."

She placed her left arm around Emma's shoulder and pulled her close. While setting her right arm on the bed, she aimed the pistol at the door. She heard voices. Male voices. She couldn't make out their words, but their tone wasn't angry or harsh.

"It could be a neighbor," she said, looking at Emma.

Emma looked up at her, tears filling her eyes. Maddie returned her gaze to the door. As frightening as all this was for Maddie, she imagined it was terrifying for Emma. Maddie had trained for things like this with Ryan and her dad.

How powerless and small Emma must feel.

Maddie resolved to teach Emma everything her dad had taught her. She was sure that Ryan and the others, when they arrived, would be glad to teach her things too. If the lights didn't come back on, Emma would have to learn those things. Better sooner than later. It could mean the difference between death and survival.

Maddie heard the screen door squeak and footsteps on the hardwood floor of the living room. She stood and held the gun in the ready position. She ran over to the door and closed it slowly. Just before it shut all the way, she heard a familiar voice.

"Maddie? Where are you, Maddie?"

Her eyes widened. Throwing open the door, Maddie ran down the hall and launched herself into her brother's arms.

Cooper ran through the open door, nosed his way between them, and put his head under Zach's right arm. Zach patted his head as he looked at his sister.

"Sis, no offense, but you look like shit," Zach said.

~

Thank you for purchasing Turbulent: Book One in the Days of Want series. The story continues in book two, Hunted. Order your copy today at Amazon.com.

If you enjoyed it, I'd like to hear from you and hope that you could take a moment and post an honest review on Amazon. Your support and feedback will help this author improve for future projects. Without the support of readers like yourself, self-publishing would not be possible.

Don't forget to sign up for my spam free newsletter at www.tlpayne.com to be the first to know of new releases, giveaways, and special offers.

~

Turbulent: Days of Want Series, Book One has gone through several layers of editing. If you found a typographical, grammatical, or other error which impacted your enjoyment of the book, I offer my apologies and ask that you let me know so I can fix it for future readers. To do so, email me at contact@tlpayne.com. In appreciation, I'd like to offer you a free ebook copy of my next book.

~

Although the people, places and events depicted in this book are fictional, the threat posed by an electromagnetic pulse or EMP is real. In January 2019, the declassified report, written by EMP expert Peter Vincent Pry, was released to the public. In it he revealed EMP war plans drawn up by Iran, Russian, China, and North Korea. In "Nuclear EMP Attack Scenarios and Combined-Arms Cyber Warfare," Pry said that "Super-EMP" weapons, as they are termed by the Russians, are specifically designed to generate an extraordinarily powerful EMP with a peak E-1 EMP field of 200,000 volts per meter which would be 100,000 volts at the margins. The U.S. has no Super-EMP weapons in its nuclear deterrent. He describes a sequencing of EMP attacks, combined with Cyber attacks aimed at crippling the nation and weakening our ability to defend the nation in such an event. His report paints a grim picture in the event of an EMP and combined-arms cyber warfare attack.

ALSO BY T. L. PAYNE

Days of Want

Hunted

Turmoil

Uprising

Upheaval

Mayhem

Defiance (Coming summer 2021)

Sudden Chaos

Gateway to Chaos

Seeking Safety

Seeking Refuge

Seeking Justice

Seeking Hope

Seeking Sanctuary (Coming soon!)

Fall of Houston

No Way Out

No Other Choice

No Turning Back

No Surrender

No Man's Land (Coming soon!)

JOIN T. L. PAYNE ON SOCIAL MEDIA

Facebook Author Page
Days of Want Fan Group
Twitter
Instagram
Website: tlpayne.com
Email: contact@tlpayne.com

ACKNOWLEDGMENTS

Many people have had a hand in the creation of this story. I am deeply appreciative for all their help and support. I'd especially like to thank my beta readers, Damon Brogdon, Chris Reid, Carol Rickets, Julie Snyder, Kathy Cornetto, Cathy Northup, Joshua Boiling, Tom Bailey, Henry Thomas, and Rebecka Perks, all of whom have provided valuable feedback on this novel. Also, a tremendous thank you to my editor and proofreaders.

I'd also like to thank you, the reader, for coming on this journey with me.

The following story is a scenario where the characters must adapt quickly to the challenging new world after such attacks. Let's all hope that this story remains fiction.

I hope you enjoy reading it. Feel free to reach out to me on social media if you have comments or questions. Join my spam free newsletter to say informed of new releases, giveaways, and special offers. I will not spam your inbox, I promise.

Best wishes,

T.L. Payne

ABOUT THE AUTHOR

About the Author

T. L. Payne is the author of the bestselling Days of Want Series. T. L. lives and writes in the Mark Twain National Forest of region of Missouri. T. L. enjoys many outdoor activities including kayaking, rockhounding, metal detecting, and fishing the many rivers of the area.